A CHRISTMAS PROPOSAL

"Yes, Philip?" she whispered.

"Just so that there's no mistake about it later . . . Are you listening, dear?"

For a moment, her heart died as she was certain he was going to tell her this was a mistake, that he'd had no intention of kissing her, that he'd only surrendered to an uncontrollable impulse.

"I'm listening," she answered warily.

"Just so that we both understand completely . . . That was a proposal."

"Oh. Was it?"

"Shall I make it more formally?"

She couldn't answer, stunned by the wonder of a moment she'd never even dreamed of except in her most secret heart.

"Camilla, I adore you. You're the woman I've sought my whole life, in every corner of the world. I never thought you existed, and here you were within fifty miles of my family home the entire time. Please, please say you'll marry me . . ."

BOOK YOUR PLACE ON OUR WEBSITE AND MAKE THE READING CONNECTION!

We've created a customized website just for our very special readers, where you can get the inside scoop on everything that's going on with Zebra, Pinnacle and Kensington books.

When you come online, you'll have the exciting opportunity to:

- View covers of upcoming books
- Read sample chapters
- Learn about our future publishing schedule (listed by publication month *and author*)
- Find out when your favorite authors will be visiting a city near you
- Search for and order backlist books from our online catalog
- Check out author bios and background information
- Send e-mail to your favorite authors
- Meet the Kensington staff online
- Join us in weekly chats with authors, readers and other guests
- Get writing guidelines
- AND MUCH MORE!

A YULETIDE TREASURE

Cynthia Pratt

ZEBRA BOOKS
KENSINGTON PUBLISHING CORP.
http://www.kensingtonbooks.com

ZEBRA BOOKS are published by

Kensington Publishing Corp.
850 Third Avenue
New York, NY 10022

All Kensington titles, imprints and distributed lines are
available at special quantity discounts for bulk purchases
for sales promotion, premiums, fund-raising, educational
or institutional use.

Special book excerpts or customized printings can also
be created to fit specific needs. For details, write or phone
the office of the Kensington Special Sales Manager:
Kensington Publishing Corp., 850 Third Avenue, New
York, NY 10022. Attn. Special Sales Department. Phone:
1-800-221-2647.

Zebra and the Z logo Reg. U.S. Pat & TM Off.

First Printing: October 2003
10 9 8 7 6 5 4 3 2 1

Printed in the United States of America

CHAPTER ONE

Camilla Twainsbury sat wedged into the corner of the public accommodation coach, her aching back braced and her elbows pressed against wall and worn leather cushion. Every so often, when she judged the motion to be slightly smoother, she'd release one arm to shove her second-best bonnet up, as it tumbled continually over her eyes.

Her mother had warned her of the rigors of travel. Her own childhood memories of frequent moves emphasized the adventurous side of things, new sights, new sounds, new friends. It seemed, yet again, that Mother was right.

Whenever Camilla pushed her bonnet up, she encountered the gaze of the dark-haired gentleman on the other side of the coach. Invariably, he'd smile at her sympathetically, his dark eyes going all crinkly at the corners. His hat had tumbled off at the first jar, but he at least could hold it on his knee without undue impropriety.

"Not too much farther now," he said comfortingly. "I recently came to live just outside Bishop's

Halt. Once you pass the Speaking Oak, it's only another few miles to the inn."

Though there was plenty of food for conversation-
sparking questions in his statements—What on
earth was a speaking oak? Who was the bishop and
why had he halted?—Mrs. Twainsbury had warned
her not to talk to gentlemen. An elderly man of mild
visage might be a permitted exception to such a
rule but not a well-spoken young man with laughter
in his eyes.

She sniffed and turned her gaze toward what little she could see of the countryside through the
smeary window. The aspect did not lend itself to
maintaining a cheerful mood. Overcast and foggy,
the sky and the landscape seemed indistinguish-
able except for the bleak skeletons of the trees.
The very sight made Camilla wish she had a large
fur muff like those she'd seen in a ladies' magazine, but her mother did not approve of fur for unmarried girls. Camilla huddled into her brown
woolen pelisse that she'd sewn herself. It had none
of the style of a modiste creation, but she'd quilted
the bodice and sleeves which helped to keep her
warm.

She stole another glance at the man who shared
the coach with her. He, too, gazed out the window,
but seemed no more impressed with the view than
she was. Dressed like any country gentleman in top
boots, leather breeches and a brown fustian coat,
he rode at his ease. The bumps and shudders of
the coach seemed not to affect him.

Camilla couldn't place him. He didn't seem to
be a professional man—neither lawyer nor doctor
and certainly not a clergyman. Nor did he seem to
be a respectable farmer or estate agent, for there
was not enough agricultural matter on his softly
gleaming boots.

During a second glance, Camilla saw that there were faded ink splatters on both of his blunt-fingered hands. Perhaps he was a schoolmaster or a tutor, but she was certain that such men were rarely so good looking.

The drumming of the horses' hooves slowed, ringing out on pavement instead of muffling dirt. "Ah, we have arrived," the stranger said. "The Red Knight Inn at Bishop's Halt."

The groom flung open the door, and the stranger hopped down as lithely as though every muscle weren't cramped from the long, uncomfortable journey. "May I assist you?" he asked, holding out his hand.

"Thank you, sir."

He chuckled. "So you can speak after all."

"When necessary."

Much more slowly than he, Camilla gathered up her few belongings. Taking his hand, she gingerly dismounted, her foot almost slipping off the little iron step, coated as it was with ice. The fresh, cold air entered her body as though it bore tiny spikes. In retrospect, the stuffy interior of the coach seemed warm and cozy.

Still holding her hand in a genial way, he turned to show her a low-roofed, white-painted inn. Two tall trees stood in the corners of the courtyard, bare now of leaves, but in summer they must have made the inn cool and welcoming. Little windows, like thatched eyebrows, nestled in the roofline, while large bay windows showed where the reception rooms must lie.

Looking around amid the bustle attendant on the arriving coach—grooms leading up fresh horses, the rooftop passengers, wind-whipped and red-cheeked, climbing down to seek the nearest fire, the hugely caped figure of the driver draining off

a steaming jug of hot punch—Camilla realized her
hostess must be waiting for her inside. Though Mrs.
Twainsbury had been unable to give her daughter
any notion of Nanny Mallow's age, surely her own
mother's nurse had to be of advanced years. No elderly lady would wait out in the cold if she didn't
have to.

"What do you think of it?" the genial stranger
asked.

"Charming. Is it yours?"

"Mine?"

"You seem as proud of it as if you had built it
yourself."

"Do I?"

Camilla took advantage of his moment of confusion to free the hand he'd unaccountably retained.
"Good day," she said, walking toward the front door.

He caught up easily. "It's interesting you should
have seen that," he said. "My ancestors had quite a
bit to do with the building of this house. You see, it
used to be an almshouse in the fifteenth century."

"How interesting. Good day."

"But before that, it was attached to an arch-
bishop's palace that used to be on that hill. It's where
the knights used to stop to polish up their armor
and whatnot before being ushered into the presence. So 'Red Knight' is really a corruption of 'Redd-
ing Knights,' you see."

"A most interesting legend. Good day."

"That's three times you have said 'good day.' I
might start to think you don't want to talk to me."

"We have a saying at home, sir. What I tell you
three times is true. Good . . ."

He started to laugh, his hands on his hips and
his head thrown back. Camilla stared at him in
alarm, sure he was suffering from some sort of fit.
None of the men she knew ever laughed like this,

from the pit of the stomach, as though laughter were some uncontrollable function.

Of course, the men she knew were older, settled, and serious. The vicar, the sexton, the doctor, and Mr. Van der Groot the apothecary were all grave men far past their first youths. Yet even the two younger men who occasionally called were not prone to laughter. Mr. Brase, estate agent, and young Jethro Fuster, only son of Sir John Fuster, discussed serious matters—like transubstantiation, philanthropism, and philosophy. Camilla sat and sewed and listened, wishing they'd use a word once in a while that she could understand. When they did recall her presence, they'd speak so slowly and with such blatantly patronizing smiles that she'd rather not know their subjects at all.

With a sideways glance at the laughing man, Camilla turned and walked swiftly into the inn. The landlord came out of a room off the main hall, wiping his hands on a dishcloth. "How may I help you, miss?"

"I'm looking for Mrs. Mallow. Is she waiting for me in the coffee room?"

"No, no women in the coffee room, miss. Ladies' parlor's the place for you."

"Where is it?" Camilla asked.

"This way." He led her toward the rear of the house and opened a door on a dusty, but quiet chamber, hung with toile curtains.

Camilla peered in. "There's no one here."

"That's right."

"Then, no one is waiting for me."

"It seems so. Would you care for some tea, miss?"

Finally a sensible question. "Very much. Thank you."

He stood there, obviously expecting her to

enter the "ladies' parlor." Camilla, always willing to do what was expected of her, began to step over the threshold. But the thought of being cooped up in a place that smelled of dust and cooking, even worse than the smell of dust and chickens which had haunted the coach, made her pause. "Is there somewhere I can freshen my appearance?"

"You'll be wanting a room?"

"Only for half an hour. After driving for so long. You understand."

The landlord's broad face showed no understanding. "We don't get many ladies at the Red Knight, miss. You'll not be wanting to spend the night?" His tone was not encouraging.

"No, I'll be staying with Mrs. Mallow. Perhaps she has mistaken the time of my arrival."

"Everyone knows when the coach comes, miss. Belike she's misread the day. Time out of mind, I've done that myself."

Camilla realized this was probably true. An old woman might easily be confused as to the date, especially as she lived in so retired a spot.

She reiterated her desire to freshen her appearance before tea, and with heavy reluctance, the landlord showed her to a small room on the next floor. He promised to send up a can of hot water as soon as someone could be spared to carry it.

Glancing in the few inches square which was all the mirror the room afforded, Camilla repressed a shudder. Her waving hair, usually so sternly controlled, had sprung forth in disordered elf locks. She flung her much-abused bonnet aside and set to repair the damage. No sooner had she ruthlessly contained her hair once more in a neat knot, than someone knocked on the door. "Water, miss," a female voice called.

"Thank you." Camilla received the maid with a

smile. She felt encrusted with dust. The maid poured out the steaming water into the basin. "I beg your pardon," Camilla said, fishing a small coin from her purse. "Do you know a Mrs. Mallow?"

"Nanny Mallow, miss? To be sure."

"Thank heaven. The landlord didn't seem to have any idea there was such a person."

"Oh, him," the maid said with a roll of her pretty brown eyes. "He don't know nothing but hunting and shooting. 'Tis the women that'd know Nanny Mallow."

"Where does she live?"

"Two miles out of town. If you be feeling ill, miss, I can run to fetch her."

"You walk there?"

"Now and then when my grandmam is feeling poorly."

"Could I find it, do you think?"

"Nanny Mallow'd come to you, miss, seeing how you're gentry."

"I'm not really. I'm supposed to be staying with her for a few weeks, but she hasn't come to meet me."

For a moment, the young maid looked troubled, but then her brow cleared. "No doubt she's off helping folks."

After drinking a cup of tea, Camilla set off to follow the maid's directions. The maid had given what sounded like excellent directions. Having lived in the country for most of her life, however, Camilla knew that the clearest directions could sometimes contain snares for the unwary. She had occasionally found herself looking for signposts that had been painted out, ponds that had dried up, and houses that had long ago burned to the ground.

Camilla repeated the maid's directions over to

herself as she came down the stairs. "Half a mile, take left-hand fork at crossroads, look for turn at medieval cross. . . ."

The man from the coach came out of the coffee room, looking over his shoulder to throw a last word into the pleased laughter of men. At the same instant, Camilla stepped down into the hall, making a sharp turn around the newel post. They collided at once.

"I'm terribly sorry," he said, grasping her shoulders to keep her upright.

For the space of a dozen rapid heartbeats, Camilla looked up into his face. Their breath mingled, and the laughter faded from his eyes. He seemed to look both at her and *into* her more deeply than anyone ever had. His fingers tightened reflexively on her shoulders.

"I beg your pardon," Camilla said, stepping back, confused and flustered. His hands fell away. "I should have been paying more attention," she said.

"Are you going out?" he asked, his eyes flicking over her body.

"Yes. I'm not staying here tonight."

"Where are you going? Not that I have the slightest right to ask you," he said, seemingly answering her thought.

Since he admitted it, she felt she couldn't point it out. "I'm not going very far, sir. I thank you for your concern."

"If you'll wait, I shall be happy to drive you wherever you wish to go. It's not fit weather for you. For a young lady, I mean."

"Thank you again, but no."

He pushed back a lock of dark hair that had fallen over his eye. "I don't blame you for not accepting. You don't even know my name. I forgot to introduce myself. I'm Philip LaCorte."

"Indeed. A pleasure, Mr. LaCorte."

"It's Sir Philip actually. I recently found myself a baronet." He smiled as though it were the sort of thing that might happen to anyone.

He didn't look old enough or distinguished enough to have garnered such an accolade through his own endeavors. "My condolences."

"And your name is . . . ?"

"I am Miss Twainsbury."

"Miss . . . Twainsbury."

"Yes." She had no intention of giving her Christian name to a chance-met stranger. Her name was her own affair.

"And you won't accept my assistance, Miss Twainsbury? My driver should have been here already. I'm sure if you'll wait with me for just a few minutes, we will soon be off."

"I am grateful for the offer, but I feel I must be on my way." Disquiet, like a cold current in an otherwise pleasant stream, ran through her, increasing from moment to moment. It was most peculiar that Nanny Mallow hadn't appeared today. Certainly there could be many reasons why she'd not come to meet her, yet something compelled her to waste no more time.

She thanked him once again as she pulled open the front door. A chill breeze blew in, skittering around Camilla's ankles like a playful cat. The freshness of the air made a sharp contrast to the fuggy heat of the inn. She heard Sir Philip inhale and sigh as if he, too, responded to the invigorating effect of the wind. "I'll come with you."

Camilla shook her head. "No, you mustn't trouble. I'll be perfectly fine."

Without waiting for him to come up with another reason to delay her, Camilla walked out, pulling the door behind her. She had hardly stepped
into the now deserted courtyard before she heard
the door open again. Glancing over her shoulder,
Camilla saw him standing in the opening, watching her. She paused, but he seemed to have nothing further to say. Throwing him a smile and a nod
which she hoped indicated her complete compe-
tency, Camilla turned away.

Her sense of urgency growing by the minute,
Camilla walked swiftly out of the courtyard, avoid-
ing as much as possible mud, water, and other ef-
fluvia.

Outside the shelter of the inn's encircling brick
walls, the wind seemed to blow with cheerful enthusiasm. She remembered seeing drawings in
books that showed the wind as a disembodied
head among the clouds, cheeks bulging with the
force of mighty exhalations. Now she understood
from where those early mapmakers took their in-
spiration.

She made certain her pelisse was closed up tight
to her throat and walked on, head down, pushing
forward against all the buffeting force of nature.
She hoped by exertion to keep herself warm, but
the hope was in vain. For all the good her pelisse
did, she might as well have been wearing light
summer muslin.

Something kept her going, however, despite the
knife-sharp cold. Stubbornness, perhaps, a sin of
which she was often guilty, or a reluctance to meet
Sir Philip's eyes while admitting defeat. She would
have to wait humbly with him until he could drive
her to Nanny Mallow's cottage. Whether he would
gloat or not, she couldn't say, but her experience

of the male sex made her think that he wouldn't be able to help himself.

As she paused at the first turn in the road, Camilla realized just how many of her mother's favorite restrictions she had shattered today. True, the edict against young ladies traveling alone had been broken by Mother herself.

When Linny's first baby had decided to arrive somewhat ahead of schedule, Mrs. Twainsbury had girded her loins and gone to offer aid, comfort, and the certainty that the task would not be satisfactorily accomplished without her presence. However, to take Camilla—young, unblemished, and innocent—into that situation passed the bounds of the permissible.

Mrs. Twainsbury had chosen the lesser of two evils and sent Camilla to the very reliable if elderly Nanny Mallow.

Since kissing her mother farewell this morning, however, Camilla had broken other rules all by herself. She'd spoken to a strange man, entered an inn quite on her own, had given the strange, if charming, man her name, and had set off on a walk entirely unaccompanied. Camilla did not know if she felt exhilarated or frightened by her temerity. Perhaps a little of both, she thought.

If at times in her life she'd felt trammeled in by her mother's rules and restrictions, she had at least always acknowledged not only Mrs. Twainsbury's right to be thus, but also the good sense of many of her dictums. What defenses did she, young and hardly intimidating physically, have except good sense, determination, and hygiene?

She breathed a deep sigh of the sharp, cold air, relishing now the metallic tang in the back of her throat. Maybe that's what freedom tasted like, she

thought wickedly. She found herself gazing with
approval at a snarling lion holding a shield, one
side of a long stone wall that ran off at an angle.
Between the lion on one side and the lamb on the
other stretched an imposing wrought-iron gate, a
padlock as large as Camilla's head hanging, sprung,
from one of the bars. Curious, for the maid hadn't
mentioned any local great house, Camilla peered
down the somewhat neglected drive. If there was
some manor down there, it was hiding behind a
grove of trees. No doubt Nanny Mallow would be
able to tell her all about the house and its inhabitants since the Year Dot.

Camilla marched on, passing the worn stone
cross that the maid had mentioned, the once-deep
carving all eroded away into a blur of half-glimpsed
animals and men. The landscape, fields and wooded
copses alike, waited under the deep silence of winter. What snow had already fallen this season had
lost its pristine whiteness in the last half-thaw, like
a threadbare blanket washed too many times. A
few ravens perched in a dry-leaved oak tree made
hoarse comments as she passed, reminding her of
the deaf old women talking about the neighbors
on the porch of her village church.

After the cross, the road gradually sank down
between banks of trees, offering some shelter from
the wind. Without that constant buffeting, she could
increase her pace.

Her muscles soon began to protest. Her mother
didn't believe in vigorous exercise for young ladies.
A gentle amble around the village green in clement
weather was quite enough to bring roses into her
girls' cheeks. Camilla never worried about her figure. Her mother also didn't believe in large meals
for young ladies.

No sooner had the wind ceased to blow than fat white flakes began to swirl down like hunks of greasy lamb's wool thrown off by a mad sheep-shearer. It was a smothering snow, a thick, floundering snow that came down in a blinding fog, withdrew and returned, bringing greater confusion. Being hit by one flake was like being struck in the face with a wet pillow. Pushing her way through many of them was as if she were being attacked by enraged mattresses.

If Camilla had not reached where the road dipped before the snow hit, she might have gone wandering off across a field and become lost. As it was, she blundered to the left, tripped over a tree root, shied, and staggered back onto the crown of the road. She stopped, catching her breath. A wild sort of fear seized her. Camilla fought off the panic, knowing she was close to her destination. "It's foolish to be frightened of a little snow," she muttered.

But in just that moment, her skirt had become entirely white. Camilla beat her hands against her thighs, shaking the caked snow loose, leaving damp and dusted fabric behind that soon became covered as before, making her skirts heavier. She realized that her feet were cramped with cold. If she did not walk on at once, she'd soon find herself cowering down in the middle of the road, covered with snow like a tree stump.

But it was hard to will herself to move on. Far easier to stand still, dazzled and mesmerized by the dancing flakes buzzing before her eyes like white bees. The cramp in her feet became a flame, driving her a few stumbling steps forward.

It seemed to take forever to walk the hundred yards of the road in the hollow. Nanny Mallow's cottage should be just a little farther beyond this point. "It might as well be on the moon," Camilla grumbled.

Just then, she heard a muffled howling. The sound cut through the cold fog, rising up to unearthly levels before stopping abruptly. Camilla staggered onward. She'd gone no more than a few steps before she heard the ululation again, dark with all the misery of the world.

Camilla could have no more refused to succor the maker of that cry than she could melt a path through the snow. She could only struggle on, her direction now determined by the howling cry.

Ahead, she spied the dim grayish outline of a building. She started toward it. At once, a dog began to bark, dry, weary barks that yet held something of joy in its tone. Camilla permitted herself to whistle, since there was no one to hear her.

She half tripped over a wooden bowl and, putting her hand out to balance herself, touched fur. A black and white dog, wet and shivering, stood next to a post sunk into the ground. The rope that tethered him was wound many times around the post until he could only move a few inches in any direction. She looked into bright brown eyes and thought, *This is a nice dog. Why would anyone leave a dog tied out in a snowstorm?*

Pulling off her gloves, she let him sniff her fingers. Despite his situation, he licked her hand, perhaps as much to taste the melted snow as to show his harmlessness. "There now," she said. "Let me just . . ."

She found the knot under his jaw. The thin rope tied around his collar was wet and seemed to have fused into a solid mass. She broke a nail and was about ready to use her teeth when a loop loosened at last. Once she'd broken the back of it, the rest came undone quite easily.

"You're free," she exclaimed.

The dog took a few halting steps, stopping at the same distance from the post he must have learned by half strangling himself every time he tried to go farther. Camilla backed up and clapped her hands, calling the dog to her. "Come on, come on, sirrah!"

The moment the dog realized he was no longer tied, he bounded away over the crust of snow, running toward the house. "You must be thirsty," Camilla said, picking up the wooden bowl and her gloves. She had to brush the snow away to find them. "I'll find you some water."

He stood outside the door, pawing restlessly at the smooth brown varnish and whining. "Stop that," she said. "You'll scratch it."

The dog danced backward, whined again, and charged at the door, leaping up to claw at the knob.

Ordinarily, Camilla would have no more walked uninvited into a stranger's house than she would have spoken to a strange man in a coach. But the freezing weather, the dog's imploring eyes, and her own increasingly miserable condition would have to explain her being so bold. Even so, she hesitated until, the wind having died for the moment, she heard a faint human cry for help.

CHAPTER TWO

The cottage had been built in a typical fashion, a series of small whitewashed rooms telescoping out from each other. She peered into the largest of them, an impeccably clean and tidy square room with a sloping chimney-breast. The mantel was crowded with mementos, bracketed by a pair of Staffordshire lovers, she in pink panniers, he waving a tricorne hat. Along one wall was a row of square windows, like the rear galley of a ship. All the curtains were open. The cold beat in remorselessly, as if there were no walls to shelter behind.

The dog pushed in ahead of Camilla, sure where she hesitated. With a yip, he ran away into one of the other rooms.

"Is anyone there?" Camilla called, following. She hoped that she'd only imagined that faint cry for help. She didn't want to face whatever caused this sense of desolation in a place meant to be cheerful and cozy.

"Who's there?" The voice, a woman's, came like a ghost's whisper, barely audible above the moaning of the wind.

"I'm Camilla Twainsbury. Where are you?" She followed the dog and found him sitting before a half-closed door. He looked over his shoulder at her, as if to ask what was taking her so long. Once again, as soon as she laid her hand on the door, he rocketed through it ahead of her.

"Oh, good boy, Rex. Good boy. I'm sorry . . . so sorry."

"Nanny Mallow?"

An elderly lady lay on the floor, her gown twisted around her. A pillow and counterpane had been pulled from the bed beside her, leaving the sheet half-drawn to the floor. The light from the net-covered window allowed Camilla to see details but not colors. She didn't need to see Nanny Mallow's color to know the older woman was in a bad way.

"How long have you been here?" she asked, dropping down on her knees beside her.

"This will be the second night. The first, I think, I was out of m'head. Thank mercy m'leg doesn't hurt the way it did before. I can hardly feel it now. But it won't bear me. I've tried."

"What's wrong with it?"

"I believe I broke it. I was reaching to knock down the cobweb in the corner and fell off the footstool like a right fool." She lifted her hand to pat her dog, lying shivering with delight near his mistress. "It's poor old Rex I felt sorry for. I could hear him crying in the yard, and there was nothing I could do for him. Be a good lass, Miss Camilla, and go to the kitchen. There's a fine fat shinbone there for him."

Her voice faded out as her eyes rolled back in her head. She slumped down, but even as she fainted, she moaned from pain. Camilla caught her by the shoulders as she fell back and laid her gently on the pillow.

"Well," Camilla said, sitting back on her heels. Her mother's old saying, perhaps passed down from the very woman before her, came into her head. "First things first. But what's the first thing?"

Her own white puffs of breath told her what to do. She found a flint and steel in the kitchen, kindled a fire there and set the kettle on, not forgetting to unwrap the butcher's bone for Rex. He drank thirstily from the bowl of water she set down on the floor. She refilled it, and he drank again. A mop and bucket in the corner reminded her of other duties.

Once she started a fire in the bedroom hearth, the cheerful glow heartened her for the unpleasant but necessary task of cleaning the floor. A quick search of a cedarwood chest on the far side of the bed discovered a treasure trove of warm blankets and a silken tie-quilt as warm and light as good white goose down could make it. Two fresh pillows under the woman's heavy head and she looked as if she lay on a very low bed.

Camilla had everything ready before Nanny Mallow's wrinkled lids fluttered. "Tea," she moaned between cracked lips. "Two days I've been dreaming of tea. . . ."

"Right here, Nanny." Camilla slipped her arm around the frail shoulders and brought the cup near. Despite her weakened condition, after a moment, Nanny Mallow held the cup herself. "Too sweet," she said, smacking her lips thirstily, "but a good cup, withal. I taught your mother how to make a good cup of tea."

"And she taught me. A clean cup, a hot pot, and boiling water." Camilla reached out to the brown-glazed teapot on a tray on the floor. "A little more? Then something to eat, perhaps? I can have this bread toasted in the twinkling of a bedpost."

"I've been lying here day and night, and I can't say I've seen 'em twinkle yet," Nanny said crisply. "But I'm most grateful to you, Miss Camilla. I'd begun to believe I'd lie here 'til spring, and a fine moldering heap I'd be by then."

"Try a little toast and then we'll see about lifting you onto the bed."

"Don't you try it, Miss Camilla. I was a dainty thing once, about your poundage, but that was long ago. If you try, you'll find the both of us lying here twisted up."

"I can't leave you lying on the floor, Nanny."

"I'm as comfortable as I'd be in my own bed. Better, for my mattress has a valley in it that would swallow a cart horse. Now that you've made me a bit more respectable, for which I'm most beholden, and a cup of tea, I don't want for anything else. Build the fire up a bit, though. I'm chilled to the marrow."

Camilla drew the silk quilt higher. "Then, shall I leave you while I go in search of assistance?"

"That's the way of it. Rex will stay with me. With a dog at my back to keep the chilblains off and that fire before me, I shall have far more than I prayed for an hour ago."

"I've never been the answer to a prayer before," Camilla said, smiling. "Where do you suggest I go? Who will be of the most help in this neighborhood?"

Nanny Mallow's face was still as wrinkled as the bark of an ancient tree, but the marks of anguish were fading. Tea seemed to be working its usual magic. When she smiled, the folds at the sides of her mouth deepened, giving her what must be her natural look, of habitual good humor and great good sense. "On your way, you must have passed the gate of a grand house."

"Yes, I saw it."

"You might as well try there first before you walk all the way back to the village. They're a handless crew at the Manor, but the oldest gel's found a bit of sense lately. More than her own mother I've thought a time or two. What do they call her? Some foolish half name . . . I never approved of shortened names. If you've a respectable name, why not use it? My own name's Priscilla, and it would take a brave lad to call me Prissy. Though there was one that did. . . ."

Fortunately, the cup that fell from Nanny Mallow's nerveless fingers was empty and bounced harmlessly on the edge of the pillow. Camilla didn't like the notion of leaving her all alone again. It was possible that Nanny had struck her head when she'd fallen. These slips in and out of awareness must have some such cause.

But when in her senses, Nanny Mallow seemed very sensible. Remaining here, though kindly comfort to the poor creature, would not serve her as well as fetching some kind of immediate aid. Even having someone to send for a doctor while she returned at once to the cottage would be a blessing. Now she wished she had accepted the gentleman's offer of a seat in his carriage. Though frivolous, he could have at least assisted her in lifting Nanny to a more comfortable surface than a hard, cold floor.

Rex returned to the room and waked his mistress with a lick on the cheek. She patted the side of his face and pushed him aside with the same motion. "Good boy; down, boy." She blinked at Camilla as if she'd forgotten her. "You're still here?"

"Yes. I didn't want to go while you were fainting."

"Why not? You could have been there already."

"I didn't want you to think I was a dream."

Despite everything, Nanny Mallow smiled. "'Twas a kindly thought, Miss Camilla. I might have at that, though Rex's breath isn't the sort of the thing a good Christian woman dreams of." Camilla could have almost given her word that Rex laughed at the joke.

"He's a very smart dog," she said. "He led me right to you."

"Fancy! He must have heard me fall. Poor old boy."

Camilla finished feeding the fire. "That should keep you warm 'til I return. Shall I leave the poker within reach?"

"Better not. If I give it a poke and a coal rolls out, I'll have the place on fire to add to my other troubles."

The last thing Camilla wanted was to go out into the snowstorm again. If it had been herself alone, she would have huddled in the cottage until it passed. But she gave only a brief thought to the warmth and shelter she was leaving. Nanny Mallow directed her toward a wardrobe where her own rough-napped cloak hung. A great muffling swathe of black fabric, it hung around Camilla like an Indian's tent. But since Nanny Mallow was much shorter than Camilla, it left her feet free.

"I'll be back as soon as I can."

"I shall await you just as I am," Nanny Mallow said with an inclination of her head that no queen could have bettered. Then her little wrinkled apple face split in a girlish grin. "Don't dawdle along smelling the posies, will you?"

"But it's such a perfectly beautiful day," Camilla said, forcing herself to answer in kind.

The wind pushed at the door so that it was hurled back all but into Camilla's face. Closing it behind her took great strength, almost more than she had. Drawing the hood forward, Camilla set out, hardly feeling the cold in her rough cloak. The snow was much deeper now, so much so that the hem of the cloak, short though it was, dragged through the accumulated drifts. If it hadn't been for the way the snow tumbled into the tops of her boots at every step, Camilla could have almost enjoyed herself.

The gates were still open. Camilla turned in, her heart lightening as she came closer to the house. She could see it through the bare trees that lined the drive, a foursquare building whose red bricks gave her hope that the warmth of the inside would match the cheerful appearance. Though her feet were heavy and her legs weary, she quickened her pace to bring her to warmth and light and assistance all the more swiftly.

When she fell to her knees between one step and the next, she almost laughed, her surprise was so complete. She had thought her journey over, and perhaps it was.

Grasping for her last reserves of strength, Camilla struggled to rise, floundering forward. Some stitches ripped free at her waist as she caught her knees in her skirts. On hands and knees, she stayed down, breathing deeply. If necessary, she could crawl to the house.

But she couldn't. Something had gone wrong with her arms and her legs. One wouldn't pull, and the other couldn't push. Hating herself, still struggling in her mind to go on despite her traitorous body, Camilla collapsed. Strange that the snow didn't seem cold on her face; rather, it felt like her favorite feather pillow at home, soft, cool, deep.

Ridiculous, she thought. *This is England. People don't freeze to death in England.*

She dragged herself forward a few more precious inches. If she had only herself to think of, perhaps she could lie here forever. But what would become of Nanny Mallow then? Goaded by this spur, she tried one last time. As her consciousness went in a flickering of dancing lights, her fingers flexed and stilled.

Philip had taken the reins from his driver for no greater reason than he enjoyed driving in the snow. The way it sprayed up under the wheels and balled beneath the horses' hooves and was thrown clear brought back memories of happier times. There should have been bells on the bridle to make a cheerful noise, but Merridew didn't approve of the extra work decorations entailed.

He took the corner into the drive smartly. "Eh, now, cautiously, young sir," Merridew the coachman croaked, gripping the brass railings on the box. Philip chuckled.

"Windy?"

"You can't blame me if I am. Feathering an edge in this weather. . . ."

"I offered to let you walk."

But he didn't regard any answer Merridew made. He had glimpsed the widespread black form lying half-hidden by snowfall. Pulling hard on the reins, he threw them to Merridew in the same instant he leapt down from the driver's seat.

"It's that girl," he said wonderingly. He looked around, trying to find some clue as to why she lay on his drive, wearing a huge cloak that he would have sworn she had not packed in either of the small bags she'd had on the coach.

"Eh? What's that?" Merridew asked. "What's that there?"

"It's a girl."

"A gypsy?"

If he'd been writing the scene, he would have answered, "No, an angel," but that was fiction. He'd liked what he'd seen of her in the coach, though she'd seemed all too prim. He couldn't commit himself to the idea of angels anyway.

When he rolled her over, snow crusted and clung to every inch of her front. The color he'd admired in her cheeks was all gone, her cheeks as pale as a drowned white rose. Her neat hair straggled in chunky wet strands. He'd seen a drowned girl once, somewhere in Upper Manhattan, during his travels in the former colonies. She'd been pushed into a millpond by a jilted lover. But that had been in the summer, and even she had not looked so cold.

With sudden panic, he settled Miss Twainsbury high against his chest and started running toward the house. She groaned, perhaps at the shaking she was receiving, and Philip ran faster, his feet understanding that she was still alive more quickly than even his head.

Merridew shouted after him. "Hoy! What about the horses?"

When Camilla came back to herself, she heard singing, high and hauntingly sweet. For a moment, she lay quite still, trying to place the tune. She was certain she knew how to play it, had practiced it a hundred times on the organ at the church, but for now the name escaped her utterly. She couldn't even grasp at the tail end of a lyric.

If she'd been fanciful, she might have imagined herself in heaven, listening to a choir of angels. However, something sharp was sticking into the calf of her left leg, and harsh fabric was scratching her cheek where it lay. Neither thing seemed to have anything to do with celestial eternity. Remembering the cool comfort of the snowbank, she couldn't help feeling that she'd changed her situation for the worse.

Camilla didn't think she had made any noise, but no sooner had she returned to consciousness than she heard someone shout, "She's awake, Sir Philip! Sir Philip! She's awake."

Fortunately, the person seemed to be moving off. Camilla heard footsteps rattle over wooden floors, and the shouting voice lessened without losing one jot of excitement. Camilla blinked and sat up, a half-finished knitted quilt sliding off her legs onto the floor. The needles still poking up through the red and green yarn told her what had been poking into her leg.

Beneath her hand, where she'd pushed upright, a fat horsehair cushion lay against the arm of a set-tee covered with blue satin. As she looked around, she saw a pleasant room, the walls a mild Wedgwood blue interspersed with panels of light satinwood. Green sprigged curtains hung over long windows, looped back to show the dreary gray of a snow-laden afternoon. An errant breeze threw a hand-ful of snow against one, and Camilla jerked with surprise. The last pin that held her hair up dropped out, letting the damp mass slide to her shoulders. The heavy touch of it against her cheek felt like vines.

Still feeling as cold as a mermaid, she stood up and walked to the fireplace, discovering some kind soul had taken off her soaked shoes. A newly kin-dled blaze giddily consumed small twigs, having not yet grown into a sober, well-fed glow among the larger logs. She held out her hands to it, feel-

ing the remaining chill drop from her skin. If only
the deep-bone chill that shook her every few moments would pass off, she'd feel as well as ever.

"You are awake."

She turned to find the gentleman of the public
coach and the inn smiling at her. "Yes," she said.
"Is this your house?"

He nodded and came into the room, half closing the door. As he did, Camilla saw that two or
three faces, some quite young, were peering into
the room behind him. She raised her hand in greeting, and for a moment, it looked as if he wouldn't
be able to keep them from swarming in. "Not yet,"
he said, quite kindly. "Let me talk to her first."

He glanced at Camilla again, then turned back,
adding, "Run along, Tinarose, and tell Cook there'll
be one more to dinner—whenever that is."

"Oh, no," Camilla said, starting forward.

"Come, you'll surely stay to eat with us. Then
Merridew will take you wherever you want to go,
though I've no doubt he'll complain mightily while
doing it. You mustn't take any notice, however. It
only encourages him."

Without quite knowing how he did it, Camilla
found herself sitting on the settee once more, the
knitted quilt again tucked around her knees. She
pushed it aside. "I'm entirely recovered, Sir Philip.
I thank you for bringing me inside, but I'm afraid
I must delay your dinner."

"You can't possibly delay it more than my cook
does."

As he was speaking, a burly young parlor maid
bustled in, the ribbons on her cap a-flying, carrying a large silver tray, burdened with a fat, gleaming teapot. Cups and saucers, little serving dishes
and eating utensils, rattled like castanets as she
walked, her steps firm and rapid. She hooked a

small table with her large foot and sent it, with a kick worthy of a rugby player, skating across the highly polished wooden floor. It stopped in front of the settee, more or less.

With an emphatic bang, she dropped the tray on the table. A few small cakes slid off their plates. "There you go," she said cheerfully. "Cuppa'll soon get the roses blooming in your cheeks, miss."

She stood there, arms folded across her significant bosom. "Well, g'wan," she said, when Camilla hesitated under this unorthodox treatment. "Set you up a treat, it will. Nobody makes a cuppa like Cook."

"It's very good of you," Camilla said with a sideways glance at Sir Philip. He didn't seem to find anything odd in his parlor maid's behavior.

"Try one o' them little pink cakes," the maid urged. "They're my favorites. She makes 'em special for me."

"Thank you for sharing them." She felt that for two pins the maid would have nudged her companionably and asked her to make some room. Having been raised to show scrupulous politeness to everyone, from the highest in the land to the most lowly, Camilla allowed no trace of her amazement to appear in her expression.

"Lawks," the maid said cheerfully, "I've been and forgot the milk. I'll be back before the cat can lick her ear." Still with resounding footsteps, the maid hurried off.

"Mavis doesn't often forget the milk," Sir Philip said, leaning forward to pour out a cup of the blackest tea Camilla had ever seen. "Usually it's the sugar. She's right, though, the little pink cakes are delicious."

Though she tried to look attentive, all Camilla's interest focused on the steam that coiled up from the Queensware cup. The savory scent of the tea wafted toward her, rich, vibrant, Indian. He smiled and passed her the cup.

Her mother and Nanny Mallow would have sneered at the tannin-thick brew. To Camilla, feeling the last shred of ice melt away from within under the pressure of the bitter, boiled liquid, it was the finest cup of tea ever created. She sighed with contentment, replacing the cup in the saucer, which, she now noticed, did not match the creamy whiteness of the Wedgwood cup. On the contrary, the saucer blazed in shades of red and blue, Imari from mysterious, cloistered Japan.

"You wanted that," he observed, reaching out to pick up the pot again.

"Yes." Restored, she recollected her duty. "Thank you, Sir Philip, for rescuing me from the snow. I may have seemed insensible, but I am aware of your kindness."

"Kindness? Not a bit of it. I merely thought you looked untidy lying out on my lawn."

She smiled at that, pushing her unruly hair out of her face. "I must impose on you further. When I reached Nanny Mallow's cottage, I found her injured."

"Injured?" he said, a small cake halfway to his lips.

"Unable to help herself. She'd fallen a day or two ago and had been lying on her floor ever since."

"Shocking," he said, his brows coming together. He put the pastry down on a plate. Dusting his fingers, he walked to the fireplace to pull a tapestry bell rope hanging there. "I leave the neighbors to Lady LaCorte," he added. "But she's been unwell of late, and I fear I have not yet taken up my full duties here. Lord of the Manor is a mantle that sits strangely on my shoulders."

Camilla knew a flare of disappointment and was ashamed of herself. She had not thought herself so shallow as to be cast down upon discovering an attractive gentleman's married state. Of course, Sir Philip must be married. A moment's reflection would have informed her reason that such a man, genteel, gentlemanly, and possessed of some fortune, must of certainty have a wife.

The parlor maid reappeared, bearing a sugar bowl cupped in her hand. "There you are, miss. Put a few spoons of that in the tea and it'll brighten your spirits. Oh, I forgot to ask if you'd care t' drop a ball o' fire in it. If you want, I'll fetch you a tot from the library."

Camilla took the sugar bowl from the maid's hand and put it next to the one already on the tray. Fortunately, she never took milk in her tea. Her mother considered it an extravagance and uncultured to boot. The reference to "a ball o' fire" confused her until Sir Philip clarified the matter.

"I don't think Miss Twainsbury cares for brandy, Mavis. Would you ask Mr. Perriflyn to come down as soon as he has finished with Lady LaCorte? Then tell Merridew to harness the horses once again. I shall need him to drive."

She nodded at him, very offhand, coming back to the point she felt was at issue. "You're certain, now, miss? Me ol' dad always said there's nothing like a drop o' brandy in tea to set you up right. Course, as time went on it was more brandy and less tea, if you catch my meaning."

"You're very kind," Camilla said, helpless under this onslaught of confidence. "I don't believe I'll indulge. Do please tell your cook how much I enjoyed her tea."

"Them cakes are a treat; didn't I tell you?"

"Yes, you did. Now if you would impress upon

Mr. Merridew—is it?" She glanced at Sir Philip, who nodded. "Impress upon him that there is some urgency in harnessing the coach. And if you would be so good as to put in a few blankets and pillows or a bolster? Yes, a bolster would be the very thing."

"I'll pass the word, miss, but Merridew ain't going to want to go out in this again. It's blowing up to be a real blizzard."

"I'm afraid it's imperative," Camilla said firmly. "Do you know Nanny Mallow?"

"Course," Mavis said, her freckled face split by a grin. She had large but fairly regular teeth. "Everybody knows her."

"She's lying in her cottage with an injury to one of her legs. We mustn't leave her there any longer than we must."

"So I'll say," Mavis said. She had whistled when Camilla had told her about Nanny Mallow, and Camilla realized the parlor maid, for all her size, couldn't be more than about fifteen years old. "Well, don't you worry no more 'bout Merridew. I'll rouse him, and if I can't, Cook'll. He can't say 'no' to her; he wants to marry her, and she ain't said she will nor she won't."

"You're undoubtedly right," Camilla said.

"And I already told Mr. Perriflyn to see to her," Mavis added with a nod toward Camilla. "I've sent m'mum up to make up a bed for you, miss. Best place for you, to my way of thinking. I told her to scorch the sheets, too."

Though a bed with warmed sheets and a hot brick at her feet sounded like the anteroom to heaven, Camilla glanced toward Sir Philip. "That was thoughtful of you, but I shall accompany the gentleman to Nanny Mallow's cottage."

"Bring Miss Twainsbury her cloak, please, Mavis. And a pair of her ladyship's boots."

Camilla smiled at him, having expected to argue the point. She hated being coddled. People, especially men, always seemed to think of her as being some fragile poppet to be protected at all costs. It was as confining as a cage and more frustrating. One could not batter at walls of courtesy, not while retaining some measure of self-respect.

"Never mind her ladyship's. I'll bring her me best boots, since hers won't never be the same. I think they shrunk a bit when we put 'em in the stove."

In keeping with the strange household, Merridew grumbled incessantly, his voice hardly muffled by the scarf he wore over his mouth. Even over the wind, rising outside the stable, Camilla could hear the constant grievance. "Interfering females, got no sense of fitness. Damn-fool woman . . ."

Sir Philip, helping with the harnesses, glanced at Camilla. "Keep it courteous, old fellow."

"Nanny Mallow couldn't help falling, Mr. Merridew," Camilla said quietly.

"Could've picked a better night for it," he said.

"She did—last night. But no one knew until today."

"All right, miss. Sure I mean no harm."

"I am sorry for the horses, though," she said, coming around to gaze at one massive roan. The intelligent eye and quick ear on the side closest to her took her measure. "It's a cold time to be driven, indeed."

"Nothing to them, miss," Merridew said gruffly. "I seen 'em play with the snow like boys out on hol-

iday." One work-twisted hand came up to tug at the
carriage horse's forelock. The other horse, seeing
this mark of favor, blew out a gust of breath reprov-
ingly. "Oh, aye, you as well," the coachman muttered
and, as if ashamed of being seen as such a soft
heart, started grumbling again.

In the carriage, as they waited for the doctor,
who ran back for a forgotten bottle, Sir Philip lowered his voice confidentially. "You must be shocked
by the free-and-easy give-and-take of the household,
Miss Twainsbury."

"Not at all, Sir Philip."

"No? Well, perhaps you wouldn't presume to
comment, but I could see shock in your eyes."

"Hardly that, Sir Philip. Showing surprise would
be as presumptuous as comment. Your household
is your own affair, and your wife's."

"A wife would be useful for many things, but not
schooling my servants. They are all old family retainers, or relations of family retainers, and not so
easily taught new manners. You haven't met Cook
yet; she's the most recalcitrant woman on earth. I
hope Merridew's wooing prospers if only to tame
him. She is uncontrollable by any earthly means."

Camilla had never known the tyranny of a loving servant; her mother did not encourage famil-
iarity, even from those who had served her longest.
"Forgive me; I must have misheard you. You did
say something about 'Lady LaCorte,' did you not?"

"My widowed sister-in-law. I'm afraid she's not
recovered from the loss of my brother and is often
unwell."

"I'm very sorry," she said, embarrassed. Could
he tell that she'd been disappointed to learn he
was married and was now pleasantly surprised to
find she'd been wrong? The doctor came, and she
couldn't pursue the subject.

They arrived at Nanny Mallow's cottage in so short a time that Camilla could hardly believe that they'd not taken some secret shortcut. She suggested it as Sir Philip opened the door.

"Not at all. It's just the difference between trudging through snowdrifts and riding over them. I haven't told you how much I admire your perseverance."

"As well you might," Camilla said with a toss of her head that made the hood slide off. Then she gave him a rather cheeky grin. "If I had made it all the way to your door. But I didn't."

CHAPTER THREE

As soon as they entered Nanny Mallow's spare room, it became obvious who was in charge of this expedition. Philip himself was ordered out almost at once as Nanny Mallow prepared herself to permit Mr. Perriflyn to make a preliminary examination. Miss Twainsbury stayed within for "I'm not so vain as to think m'beauty's going to overwhelm you, Mr. Perriflyn, but people do gossip so."

When Perriflyn came out, they could hear Nanny Mallow giving Miss Twainsbury orders. Perriflyn laughed a little, hoarsely. "I don't think she's broken anything. Merely a bad sprain of the knee, very painful, however. Elderly women don't fall well; she's fortunate not to have broken something. She is also slightly dehydrated and more than a little hungry, but some decent meals will soon set her up again."

"I feel some guilt knowing she lay there for two days before anyone found her."

"These things happen," Mr. Perriflyn said with a sigh and a shake of his head. "Even in large cities where every neighbor lives cheek by jowl, let alone in small hamlets like Bishop's Halt."

"Can she be moved? I'd like to take her back to the Manor."

"Absolutely. I should recommend it even if she had done less of an injury than she has."

"Very well. Will you tell Merridew we'll be leaving in a few minutes?"

Philip went into the bedroom. Miss Twainsbury scurried around in her too-large boots, collecting various items to fold hastily and place into a valise under Nanny Mallow's instructions. For a moment, Philip took an overwhelming interest in the ceiling rather than observe the mysterious underpinnings of Nanny's attire that Miss Twainsbury flourished. Once Nanny gave orders to move on to the outer clothing, Philip went to kneel beside her.

"For someone who has been lying on the floor for two days, you look remarkably healthy," he said. He absently fondled Rex's bent-tip ears.

"That's not saying much," Nanny replied tartly. "But I feel better now that all of you are here. It was being on my own, with never a soul come by me, that made me feel so low."

"You can hardly complain of neglect now," he said. "We'll have you out of here and in a comfortable bed. Before you know it, all this will seem like a bad dream, popped like a soap bubble upon waking."

"Oh, what about Rex?" Nanny asked.

"He is more than welcome to come to the Manor," Philip said, "providing he stays out of my sister-in-law's apartments. Lady LaCorte is still unwell."

"She should bestir herself and take exercise daily," the older woman said tartly. "I've never believed in wrapping women up in cotton wool. Our strengths aren't like a man's, thank mercy; but we've our own power, and letting it waste away doesn't do anyone a particle of good. Never mind the stays, dear. I don't think I'll have much use for them."

At last the packing was done. Merridew gladly seized the valise and stomped out. "Poor man," Nanny said. "Some there are who can't stand the sight of pain in others."

"I'm one of them," Philip said with a smile, coming over to kneel beside her. "I do hope I won't hurt you too much."

"You're not the kind to walk away," she said somberly. "If you hurt me too bad, I'll not be shy about telling you so."

"I know Mr. Perriflyn brought laudanum," Miss Twainsbury said. "Perhaps a composer to make you feel more the thing?"

"Now that's something I don't hold with," Nanny countered. "Not when my head's not clear."

"That's what Sir Philip said when I suggested it," Mr. Perriflyn said glumly.

"I have some experience with injured persons," Philip added, hoping neither woman would think him utterly incompetent.

"Hmph. If it's all the same to you, Mr. Perriflyn, I'd just as soon have the doctor cast his eyes over me. Not that I don't trust you; it's only that I'm used to Dr. March's ways. He's very nearly as good as his dear old father was."

"I'll send Merridew for him as soon as we've got you home," Philip promised.

"Wait 'til Nanny and I are inside before you tell him," Miss Twainsbury said. "His language will be something appalling, I'm sure."

Philip was struck anew by the contrast between

Miss Twainsbury's voice and her eyes. Her voice, though pleasing enough for a girl, neither too sharp nor too low, never changed very much. The inflections and cadences remained placid, cool, and colorless. Her eyes, however, snapped, twinkled, and laughed. They expressed a thousand shades of meaning to which her voice never gave a clue.

They were pretty eyes, too; brown shot through with amber lights. Slightly almond-shaped between rows of lengthy lashes, they gave an exotic touch to an otherwise typically English face: good skin, slightly round cheeks and chin, and ash blond hair springing rather wildly from a hastily devised knot on the back of her head. He believed Miss Twainsbury, for whatever reason, worked quite hard at remaining unanimated, but she was betrayed time and again by her expressive eyes.

"Is the fire out in the kitchen, dear?" Nanny Mallow asked.

"I'll check again," Miss Twainsbury said.

Whereas Philip had felt strong and alive while carrying Miss Twainsbury into his house, gathering up Nanny Mallow gave him the sensation of being a callous brute. The more he tried to carry her gently, without jarring her injured leg, the more obvious her attempts to conceal her pain became. It was undoubtedly a relief to them all when she fell unconscious before he'd carried her all the way through the main room of the cottage.

"Has she done this before?" Perriflyn asked.

"Yes, several times," Miss Twainsbury said, hurrying to cradle the gray head before it knocked into the door frame.

"Not good," the apothecary muttered.

"Does the doctor live far?" Miss Twainsbury asked.

"I don't like these spells of fainting any more than you do."

"Perhaps it's better this way for now," Philip said, his boots crunching through the snow. It came up to their tops, and some sifted in. "I'd rather she be unconscious and out of pain during the carriage ride. The road isn't going to be good."

Merridew had opened the carriage door, though he'd then climbed back onto the box. His breath and the horses' steamed like fog in the frigid air.

After they'd tucked her carefully into the carriage, wrapping her round with blankets and propping her into the corner with the fat round sausage of a pillow that Mavis had dredged up, Mr. Perriflyn climbed in, sitting beside Nanny to hold her upright.

Miss Twainsbury hesitated before entering. "The dog?" she asked, turning back.

"Oh, yes. Come on, boy," Philip called. "Come on."

Rex danced forward, one ear inside out, flipped over the top of his square head. While Philip called to him again, patting the carriage step, he wiggled backward, forefeet splayed out in the snow, his back end higher than the front. He seemed perfectly willing to join in this game, as soon as someone explained the rules to him.

"Come on, ye daft beast," Merridew called. "It's cold as a witch's—"

"Merridew!" Philip said crossly, and the coachman folded his arms across his chest and stared off into the silent afternoon. The snow muffled every sound; even their voices sounded muted.

"Maybe if we drive off, he'll follow," Mr. Perriflyn suggested, tucking his thin hands into his armpits.

One glance at Miss Twainsbury's vividly reproving eyes and Philip made up his mind.

Climbing down, he approached the dog slowly, his hands spread out at his sides. "Good boy," he said soothingly. "Time to get in the carriage."

Rex looked at him out of one eye, his head tilted to one side. Philip came closer and closer. Then Rex dashed left. Philip swerved right and came down full-length in the snow. With a cheerful bark, Rex scampered over the snow and, hip-hop, into the carriage.

Rising up on his hands, spitting to clear his mouth, he glared across to where Miss Twainsbury choked, her gloved hand tight over her enchanting mouth.

Philip tried to look angry but couldn't resist the smile that took over his control. "Funny, is it?" he demanded. With deliberate speed, he stood up, bringing with him a double handful of snow which, while holding her gaze, he compacted into a ball.

"Sir Philip," she said warningly. She reached to one side, still keeping her watchful gaze fixed on his, and scooped some snow off the fender.

For an extended moment, they stood, weapons at the ready. Even Merridew made no comment. Then, recollecting that this young woman was a stranger and gently born, Philip let his snowball drop, where it instantly blended into that already fallen. Her eyes still twinkling, Miss Twainsbury did the same. "You are right, sir. It isn't really the time for frolicking."

"I shall challenge you again, by and by."

"I shall accept," she said with a proud tilt of her chin. Her head still up, she entered the carriage without another word.

Philip stood by, his hand on the door until she was seated. "Merridew, drive with extra care."

"You don't have to tell me that," came the grumbling answer.

"No, I don't, do I? After we reach the Manor, you'll have to go bring Dr. March."

"Aye-aye, sir," Merridew said without further complaint.

The lurch as the carriage set off was hardly perceptible, yet Nanny Mallow groaned. "Was it wise to move her?" Miss Twainsbury asked. "Wouldn't it have been wiser to bring the doctor to her home?"

"She couldn't stay there alone in any case," Philip said.

"I would have stayed with her."

"Are you experienced as a sick nurse? You would have to do everything for her, and you are not strong enough to lift her. There are many unpleasant details associated with the sickroom that a young lady cannot be expected to—"

"I have nursed my mother through a bad bout of grippe," she answered as though applying for a position. "Believe me, Sir Philip, no one could be a more demanding patient than Mother. Who will care for Nanny Mallow at the Manor?"

"Mavis's mother is an accomplished nurse," he said.

Mr. Perriflyn brightened. "Mrs. Duke? An excellent choice."

"She has helped my sister-in-law through all four of her confinements."

"Four? Then, those children I saw today are your nieces and nephews?"

"Only nieces," Philip said, hoping his rue wasn't too apparent. Mr. Perriflyn was a notorious gossip. Half his patients called him in only to hear the details of every other one's life. "Else there would be some other baronet installed at the Manor, even if only a very young one."

"Oh, of course," she said. "How stupid of me."

"How could you know?" he asked reasonably. She didn't pursue the conversation. Someone must have told her once to be seen and not heard and she'd taken the censure to heart. Or perhaps she noticed how Mr. Perriflyn's gaze flickered between them in fascination. Any innocent word or gesture could be twisted into something greater than a first meeting's delicate give-and-take. He didn't even know her given name.

Nanny Mallow raised her head from where it rested on Mr. Perriflyn's buckram-padded shoulder. "How long does it take to reach the Manor, anyway? I could have walked it by now, bad leg and all."

"It has taken rather longer than I expected," Philip said.

After suggesting that the others bundle up as warmly as possible, Philip lowered the top panel of the window. "Merridew?" he shouted up at the driver. "Is there a problem?"

"None, sir, but that a tree fell 'cross the road. I'm going by Shallcross."

"Very good. Carry on."

He closed the window and turned to the women. "The snow will be bringing down trees all over these valleys. It's so heavy and we've had such a dry fall, there's nothing for the roots to cling to."

The coach shook and swayed as Merridew fought for every foot of road. Rex, huddled on the floor, kept his thoughtful brown gaze fixed on his mistress, only occasionally casting a glance at Philip. He had no difficulty interpreting that look, despite the difference in their species. It was reproachful, full of disappointment that he, one of the Lords of Creation, couldn't do a better job. Except for a few minor details, it was identical to the look Mr. Perriflyn kept giving him.

Miss Twainsbury bore up uncomplainingly, never even to the extent of a mournful glance, despite a return of the bluish tinge around her mouth and a tendency for her soft pink lips to quiver. Philip wondered at himself. It wasn't like him to notice things like that.

In spite of Mr. Perriflyn's flapping ears, Philip committed himself as the temperature in the carriage continued to drop. "There's no doubt, Miss Twainsbury, that you will pass at least this one night under the Manor roof."

"I'm afraid you are right. I haven't anywhere else to go, have I?"

"Not that I can see. The inn is very fine, but hardly fitting for a young lady."

"Very well," she said, folding her hands. "It's the only sensible thing to do."

Rex was the first out of the carriage as they arrived at the Manor. He gave one bark to show his appreciation, then set off, his nose close to the ground. Snuffling up the snow made him break stride, sneezing.

Merridew came up to the door. "These beasts are done," he said bluntly.

"Then please saddle Paladin and Icarus."

"Two?"

"I'll have Perriflyn ride home and then I'll bring the doctor back on Icarus. Riding horses will get through where carriage horses cannot."

"But young Dr. March goes in fear of horses. He can't ride," Merridew said in protest.

"Well, it's a grand day for learning, don't you think?"

* * *

Rather soggily, Camilla squelched up the staircase behind Sir Philip, who carried the now awake but silent Nanny Mallow. The Manor had the air of a house that had settled peaceably into middle age. The walls could have used a new wash of distemper, but the mellow biscuit color flattered the white-painted woodwork. The carpet runner was a trifle worn over the edges of the steps, but not seriously so. Yet there were fine paintings on the walls, and several tables interspersed down the length of the hall bore ornaments Camilla felt she'd like to investigate. The combination confused her.

To Camilla, used to scrubbing and painting their smaller home every spring in a rigorous regime, as well as dusting daily with great care the curiosities her mother kept locked up the rest of the time in a tall cabinet, it seemed both comfortable and welcoming.

With no more introduction than "Miss Twainsbury, my niece, Tinarose," Sir Philip laid his burden on the bed and left on his mission.

Mavis had just that instant withdrawn a gleaming brass bed warmer from between the sheets. She laid it on the hearth and crept closer. "Who's that?" Nanny asked crisply. "Mavis? Mavis Duke?"

"Yes'm," Mavis said, strangely cowed.

"Well, don't stand there, girl. Help me off with m'bonnet."

"Yes'm."

Camilla turned to the other girl as she turned aside from the fireplace, hanging up the bellows with which she'd been encouraging the flames.

"How do you do, Miss LaCorte?"

The girl's dark eyes flashed over her in one all-encompassing glance. "What did Uncle Philip say your name was?"

"Twainsbury; Camilla Twainsbury. I'm a friend of Nanny Mallow's."

"Oh, you must be the one who found her. Mavis told me."

"That's right."

"I'm glad you did," Tinarose said with a sudden smile. "We all like Nanny Mallow, but we're not often allowed to go see her. My mother . . ." She caught herself before she could utter a criticism. Even in the dimness of the bedroom, Camilla could see the color that stained her cheeks.

"Certainly not in the middle of a snowstorm, I'm sure." Camilla approached the fire, holding out her hands to the blaze. "Goodness, I'm cold sheer through. I don't think I've been out in weather like that since I was a little girl. My father used to take us sledding down the big hill behind our house in Devon."

"Merridew says it'll blow over by tomorrow. My sisters are hoping for a white Christmas."

Nanny's croak came from the bed. "A white Christmas means a white spring."

"What's that?" Tinarose asked. "A white spring?"

"Weddings, child. Many weddings. And after, many children. I only hope I'll be there to see it."

"And why not?" Camilla challenged. "You heard Mr. Perriflyn say that there wasn't much the matter—merely a sprain."

"It's not the same when you're old," she said, her voice shaking. Camilla realized that now Nanny Mallow felt herself to be safe and cared for, she could give in to the fear that she had fought so valiantly while lying alone in her cottage.

Before the tears she saw in Nanny Mallow's eyes could slip over the wrinkled cheeks, she turned to the other two girls. In the light of the candles beside the bed, she saw that they were of an age, Tinarose

LaCorte perhaps only a year or so older than her servant.

"Mavis, will you fetch Nanny's valise? I last saw it in the entry hall. And if you would, could you ask someone to bring up some hot water for tea?"

"Tea," Nanny Mallow sighed, as if offered a ticket into heaven. "Did I tell you to pack my herbs and infusions, Camilla?"

"No, but I'm sure someone here has some of your making. Am I right, Miss LaCorte?"

"I might know where to put my hand on some," Tinarose said with a sideways glance and half a smile. She was pretty in her youth and health, though her nose was too long for beauty and her eyes bore dark circles. The unadorned frock of a schoolroom miss did nothing to increase her charms. With her dark hair and slightly olive skin, she would have been dramatic and fascinating in deep red. But even when she made her debut, such shades would be forbidden to her.

"Let's be about it, then," Camilla said, dismissing her troop.

Before the girls returned, Mavis's mother came bustling in. Shorter even than her half-grown daughter, she bore herself with great pride, her black hair as elaborately set and curled as any grand lady making her curtsey before the king.

"If I'm not wanted, Miss . . ." she began as soon as she put her foot over the threshold.

"Don't be so daft," Nanny Mallow said with a return of spirit. "I can't help myself, so there's only you to do it. You're almost as good a nurse as you think you are, so get on with it. And you . . . ," she said, catching Camilla's hand. "There's no words under my tongue to tell you what my gratitude is."

"Hush now. . . ."

"No, people should speak of such things. I owe

you much and what I owe I pay. Now along with you. Tell one of those girls to fill you a bath and get out of those wet boots before you catch your death."

Suddenly, as the image of a brass tub appeared in her mind, complete with curls of steam rising from the verbena-scented depths, Camilla couldn't bear her damp and bedraggled condition another instant. Pausing only to squeeze Nanny Mallow's hand, she hurried to the door. "Oh, please, which room is mine?"

"You might as well take the one next door," Mrs. Duke said grudgingly. "It's not as fine as this, but considering you're a lady born and not an old witchwoman, it'll have to do."

"Save the soft words, you old besom," Nanny Mallow said, "and come over here to get me out of these clothes. Youngsters don't need to see what they'll be coming to by 'n' by."

A peek in the room next door was not encouraging. No fire, no warming pan, and a slight smell of mold made it seem dank and neglected. By the light of the low-held candle in her hand, she caught a glimpse of her reflection. Pale, drawn, with tangles of hair falling snakily about her face, she looked like a bloodless ghost. She also bore a stain of mud on the bodice of her dress, large enough to run over her like a sash. Camilla decided to search for a warmer corner before she made repairs.

It was in her mind that if she hurried, she could regain her presentability before Sir Philip returned home. She didn't want his next impression of her to be that of the dilapidated Gorgon she saw before her.

"Vanity, all is vanity," she said and sneezed twice. Still squinching along in her too-large, damp boots, Camilla sought the warmer regions below stairs. Of course in this unconventional household, she did not know what she would find. Anything from bacchanalian revels to a quiet spot of tree worship, she imagined.

The house breathed quietly. A pleasant scent like fresh flowers filled the air, odd in winter. As she walked down the stairs, the scent was slowly replaced by that of baking apples. Her mouth watered as she realized how long it had been since she'd eaten. Except for a little pink cake, she'd not tasted anything substantial since the slice of bread and butter with which she'd started her day. Hard to believe that it had only been this morning that she'd left her home.

If the Manor were anything like Sir John Fuster's house in her own village, the door to the servants' quarters should be under and behind this staircase. She made a sharp turn, and to her pleased surprise, the green baize door was exactly where she'd surmised.

In Mrs. Twainsbury's phrase, it was not "done" for a lady to enter another house's servants' quarters without the express permission of and possible accompaniment of the hostess. But the beckoning fragrance of baked apples was impossible to resist, and Camilla did not hesitate to push open the door. A deep voice upraised in song, so deep that she wasn't certain at first if it was a man's or a woman's, reached her along with a stronger scent of cinnamon and cloves.

"And the judge laid down, with a fearful frown, the sentence from on high; Allen Ramsay must die, must die. Yes, Allen Ramsay must die!" The last high note told her the singer must be woman, or that a great tenor was lost to the stage.

"Hello?" she called, penetrating further.

"Who's that?" the voice said, breaking off in mid-verse, something about a maiden's tears.

"It is I. Miss Twainsbury."

"Oh, is it, then? Come. Let me get a good look at you."

CHAPTER FOUR

"Well, if it isn't the heroine of the hour," the cook said, turning like a battleship to unmask her guns. Her dazzlingly white apron would have made a fine mainsail, a yard long and twice as wide. It was tacked to a bosom that would have done any bowsprit proud below a pair of shoulders that any able-bodied seaman would have squared with pride. A drop of sweat glistened on the woman's brow, sliding down from iron-colored hair bound and wound about with dozens of elaborate braids.

Camilla had never met with so much hostility in her life as she'd found at the LaCorte Manor. She was beginning to worry that her own behavior was somehow calling forth this reaction. Yet she couldn't remember any pride or arrogance on her part that would account for it.

The guns did not fire. The cook swept her hard eyes over Camilla, and if her expression did not soften, her tone altered. "You're not old at all, are you? That Mavis told me you was an old lady."

"It's this hairstyle," Camilla said, smiling as she

dragged a damp hunk off her cheek. "It makes me look more mature."

A smile twitched the corner of the down-drawn mouth. The cook stretched out a brawny arm, heavy with muscle from beating batters and hammering cuts of meat wafer-thin. Hooking a finger around a sturdy chair, she pulled it in front of the massive blackened iron stove.

"Sit ye down," she ordered. "Take off them clod-hoppers of Mavis's and get warm."

Camilla obeyed.

With the side of her hand, the cook slapped open one of the iron portals of the big stove. As though a dragon had opened its mouth, the roaring and rattling of the fire in the chimney filled the kitchen. The flames, orange and bright yellow, snapped like the banners of hell's army while heat, blessed heat, wrapped around Camilla.

Slowly, she moved to obey the cook's commands, wiggling off the boots and the thickly knitted woolen stockings while the woman's back was turned.

A moment later, the cook was lifting her feet and placing them in a round, flat copper basin. A heaping tablespoon of mustard went in followed by a stream of hot water from a high-held kettle.

Camilla sank against the back of the chair as the cold retreated from the cloud of steam that enveloped her. Inch by inch, the chill of her bones was chased away. Between the mustard footbath and the dragon's breath from the stove, she felt as if she were melting. Soon nothing would be left but a grateful puddle.

But the cook's treatment wasn't complete.

Camilla found a tall, curve-sided mug in her hand, the most delicious aroma arising from the sludgy-looking liquid. She could have sworn something went "plop" in the depths, as the dark brown liquid roiled. There were yellow flecks of butterfat amid the frothing milk on the top.

She looked doubtfully into the mug, then glanced up at the cook. Standing over her with her arms crossed, deep-dimpled elbows showing under the rolled-back sleeves of her day dress, the cook gave a brief, but encouraging nod. Even more encouraging, however, was the beguiling fragrance beckoning to Camilla's taste buds.

With a hesitation that did not last beyond the first sip, Camilla tasted the hot cocoa. Mixed with cinnamon, cardamom, and other spices that danced on her tongue, it was a taste more blissful, or sinful, than any she had ever tried. She opened the eyes she had not realized she'd closed to savor the exquisite blend of chocolate and spice. "Amazing," she said. "What's in it?"

"A pinch o' this 'un and a dash o' that. 'Tis a family receipt."

"My compliments to you."

She nodded regally, a goddess on her own hearth. "Puts the pink in your cheeks." Slapping her side with a noise like a fish flapping on the water, she smacked her lips. "Puts the flesh on, too. Need it, this weather."

"I suppose so." Camilla looked down into the mug. The level of cocoa had already dropped significantly, and she hadn't even realized how much she'd drunk. "Good heavens," she said, undoing the top button of her woolen dress. "I'm already feeling ever-so-much warmer."

The cook judged her again with narrowed eyes. "Not yet." She picked up a log from the wood basket and pitched it easily into the open stove. The flames licked up even higher. "Don't get up. Have another."

The cocoa in the chocolate pot didn't pour; it

blupped out, stopping and starting as rich lumps of chocolate caught and were released through the narrow spout. Camilla had practically to chew her way through her second portion. Dinner, which had seemed of such desperate interest, suddenly retreated to the mildest of curiosities. With cocoa like this, she didn't care if she ever ate dinner again.

After a few more swallows, the cook gave her a towel to dry her steaming hair. It seemed curlier than ever before. Camilla wasn't sure if it was the combination of steam, heat, and the quick drying, or the cocoa. If it put roses in her cheeks and meat on her bones, mightn't it make her hair curl?

She couldn't help but undo her second button. Though now more than warm, she felt too enervated to move. The very idea of entering that chilly bedroom was more than she could face. She felt like a child again, retreating to the kitchen where, provided you didn't make too much noise, you'd be left in peace to read, to steal an apple or two, and to eavesdrop on fascinating servant gossip.

Thinking of those carefree hours, Camilla laid her head back against the top of the chair, lassitude invading her every atom. Perhaps she slept a little, for she suddenly found herself listening to voices even while aware they'd been speaking unintelligibly in the background of her dreams for some time.

"—that lost-lookin', like she'd been dragged backward through a hedge and no more color to her face than you'd find on a sheet of paper."

Camilla recognized the grunt that followed. Merridew was in the kitchen. "Foolhardy courage," he said. "The captain would know what to say to her, I reckon."

"Miss Tinarose would've done the same," Mavis chirped. "If her mother'd let her go."

"Don't say anything 'gainst her la'ship," the cook warned in a low growl.

"I ain't. Just . . . Miss Tinarose never seems to get her chance."

"Wants to be found facedown in a blizzard, does she?" Merridew scoffed. "Though' she was a downed tree, at first. Or a drowned dog. She sure looked as good as dead when he brung her into the house."

It was a good thing, Camilla thought, that she had no exaggerated notion of her looks. Otherwise all these compliments would swell her head. She decided to make herself known, before their comments grew any more commendatory. Next they'd be congratulating her on being marginally less gargoylelike than they remembered.

She shifted in her chair, kicking a little water out of the basin before she remembered her feet were in it. "Oh, I'm sorry," she said.

"Mavis . . . ," the cook said.

"All right, all right."

The towel Camilla had used to dry her hair had fallen across her lap when she'd drifted off. Now, carefully lifting her feet from the water, she let Mavis drag the basin aside and then reached down to start drying them. She felt a little dizzy and had to stop.

"Mavis . . . ," the cook said again.

"Never you mind, miss," Mavis said, running the mop over the spilled water. "I'll dry 'em for you."

"Thank you, Mavis, but I'll take care of my own feet." Feeling that she had been a little ungracious, she added, "Thank you for the loan of your boots. They kept me beautifully dry."

"Don't mention it."

Camilla turned now to see the cook and Merridew watching her. They sat at the big kitchen table which had been scrubbed so often the wood was worn white. Yellowish bone dominoes splayed across the service, a great untidy pile. "Who's winning?" she asked brightly.

"I am," the cook said, as if it were too commonplace an occurrence to discuss.

"She always wins," Merridew said, glancing at the woman across from him. For an instant, Camilla saw in his tired old eyes a flash of wonder, all mixed with pride. He seemed unable to believe that the marvelous creature across from him could spare him so much as a thought, let alone deign to play games with him. As soon as he saw Camilla looking at him, he frowned and cleared his throat shatteringly loud.

She turned again to Mavis. "How is Nanny Mallow?"

"They were quarreling like a new cat and an old dog," the parlor maid said. "Never thought I'd live to see the day someone could outtalk Mum. But that Nanny Mallow never stops long enough to draw breath, let alone get her thoughts in order. The words just come spilling out, like water from a downspout."

"She looked so wan and drawn," Camilla said. "She should have quiet."

"Oh, I reckon Mum'll start using silence on her soon enough. But don't worry none, miss. Mum's a good nurse; she'll see to it Nanny Mallow gets better. She's got her pride, same as anybody."

"That's right," the cook said.

Camilla put her hand to her head and found that her hair was all but completely dry. Pushing it back, her fingers tangled in it. She had no need to glance in a shiny pot bottom to see herself. Her hair had become one great knot at home on two or three occasions, and it had taken hours of eye-watering effort from her mother to return all to smoothness. "I hope I shall be able to get the knots out without cutting it," she said to herself.

She thought about getting up to brush her hair, to sponge her dress back into respectability, and again to pull on the uncongenial boots. But she felt too boneless to move. When the cook removed a dish of baked apples from a side compartment of the stove and laid it on the table, Camilla couldn't even muster the energy to ask for one. Actually, after two cups of the cook's chocolate, she felt as a South American boa constrictor must feel after swallowing a small pig, but the scent of cinnamon, clove, and apple would have tempted a monk sworn to austerity to climb down from his pillar to demand a taste.

It brought Sir Philip instead. He opened one side of the double doors at the far end of the kitchen. Camilla caught a glimpse of a passageway made of glossy beige bricks behind him. He must have hung his greatcoat up in the passage, but snow still crusted his boots. He stamped twice upon the mat to remove it.

"What's that smell?" he asked, sniffing the air like a hound catching a scent. "Baked apples? I adore 'em."

"They're for the nursery tea," the cook said.

"What, all of them? Are we feeding children or baby elephants?" Then he saw Camilla, and a bright smile took over his face, replaced an instant later by concern as he walked up to her. His cheeks were red from cold. "Miss Twainsbury, you look all in. Hasn't anyone in all this great house offered you a place to lie down?"

She noticed that both Merridew and Mavis had become very busy with his entrance. Merridew was scraping up all the dominoes and replacing them in their rosewood box. Mavis had seized a mop and immediately attacked the wet footprints Sir Philip had made.

"I'm very well, thank you. Everyone has been so kind. Nanny Mallow is resting. Mrs. Duke is with her."

"Yes, the doctor has gone upstairs. I simply came in this way after seeing to the horses."

"Eh?" Merridew interjected. "What's that?"

"They're well bedded down for the night. Now for you, Miss Twainsbury. . . ."

"I should be glad of a stable," she admitted. "Though your cook has taken excellent care of me, as indeed everyone has."

"Mum's likely got the other room ready for you, miss."

As no one seemed to notice her bare feet or her reluctance to move, Camilla felt it incumbent upon her to make an effort. Anything was better than sitting here helpless while Sir Philip stood over her. He had praised her courage, which had been unexpectedly sweet. She didn't want to endanger that good opinion, since everyone else seemed to be reserving judgment.

"Mavis," the cook said. "Show Miss Twainsbury upstairs, then come right back, mind."

"I'll show Miss Twainsbury the way," Sir Philip said. "You've work to do."

"She can do it," the cook urged.

"'At's right," Merridew added. "Lazy little thing. Do 'er some good t'trot up them stairs."

"I don't mind, Sir Philip, 'deed I don't."

He held up his hand. "Nonsense. It's my pleasure." He bent his arm and offered it to Camilla. Surprised by the eagerness the servants had shown to assist her, she wondered if accepting her host's arm was some breech of etiquette. Nevertheless, she took it.

"Thank you. I am rather tired."

"Not surprisingly so," he said, leading her toward the kitchen door. A frown contracted his brows. "Pardon the personal suggestion, but . . . Have you shrunk, Miss Twainsbury?"

"In the wet?" she asked, laughing. "No, I don't think so."

He glanced down at her bare toes. Foolish to blush but she couldn't help it. The hot blood washed into her cheeks. "I . . . ?"

Without a word or any sign of effort, he bent and swept her up to settle high against his chest. A yip of surprise escaped her. "Sir . . ."

"I carried you in from the snow," he said. "What's the difference now except it's easier if you're awake. Arms around my neck, please. It helps redistribute the weight."

She obeyed, her eyes still wide. His coat collar and cravat were still slightly damp as were the sides and back of his hair. She'd never been so close to a man before. She could see that his eyes were not all dark gray as she'd supposed. A rich brown ringed each pupil in an unusual and attractive combination. His eyebrows came rather far down his face, so that they ran from the bridge of his nose quite to the outside corner of his eye. She felt, now that she looked closely, that this partially accounted for his expression of good humor.

He noticed that she was looking at him curiously. "No doubt you are wondering about our circumstances," he asked.

"I hope I'm not so impertinent." She tried to forget about the strength of the arms under her body and the support of his hand on her back. Though she felt every instant that she should fall, she could not recall being so comfortable before.

"Nothing impertinent about it. You find yourself, willy-nilly, involved with us." With her silence, he continued, seeming to have no trouble with his breathing. "I inherited the property from my elder brother, Myron. He was captain aboard His Majesty's three-decker, *Gauntlet*. Six months ago, sailing in Philippine waters during a hurricane, he was washed overboard."

"How dreadful," she said. The usual formula, she feared, but she hoped he realized her sincerity. "One expects to hear of the loss of gallant men during wartime, but now with peace. . . ."

"I believe that the men who sail in our ships are always at war, if not with other nations, then with the sea herself. All too often, the victories go to the waters."

"It must have been a great shock to his wife, I'm sure."

"All the more so since he'd been home on leave for more than a year. They had hardly ever been together so long in all their married life, so of course she came to rely on his strength very greatly. To have that prop taken away was bitter, but to know now that it can never be renewed is almost too much for her strength of mind. Beulah is rather delicate at the best of times, and now, in her present state . . . That is . . ."

The door behind him swung open, and instantly Camilla saw what Sir Philip had hinted. The woman in the doorway had a figure that noticeably swelled in the center. Not tall, she had impeccable posture that dared one to notice her pregnancy.

"And who is this?"

It was impossible for Camilla not to feel yet again the implacable hostility that she'd met everywhere in this house, save from Sir Philip and Tinarose. She felt the puppyish Mavis hardly counted.

She couldn't really see the woman's eyes with the light coming from within the room, but the note of severe dislike sounded even more clearly than in the voices of the servants.

Camilla couldn't understand it. She'd done nothing; she didn't even know these people. Could they be mistaking her for someone else? But why, then, wouldn't they call her by some other name so she might correct their misapprehension?

"How do you do, Lady LaCorte?" she said, acutely aware that her position in Sir Philip's arms demanded explanation, yet determined not to be the one to offer it. "I'm Camilla Twainsbury."

"Camilla," Sir Philip said softly in her ear. Perforce, she glanced at him and found him smiling. "I'd wondered," he said. "All you said to me was 'Miss Twainsbury.' "

"I hope I didn't say it like that," Camilla said, objecting to his rather sniffy imitation.

A tapping reminded them that they were not alone. Camilla looked down and saw that Lady LaCorte's foot was twitching impatiently beneath the hem of her day dress. "I understand from my daughter that you have been instrumental in rescuing Mrs. Mallow from some misadventure or other."

Camilla responded to this challenging statement with nothing more than a nod. It seemed safest somehow.

Lady LaCorte came out of the doorway. Her mourning clothes were profoundly black, made of some dull, heavy silk that didn't even glimmer, nor did it rustle. "Let me see if we've made you sufficiently comfortable."

She swept along before them. Camilla glanced with half a frown into Sir Philip's face. At first, he seemed slightly perturbed, watching the slow gliding figure of his sister-in-law. Then, feeling Camilla's gaze upon him perhaps, he met her eyes and threw her a quick wink.

Lady LaCorte was hardly as tall as Camilla herself, but she bore herself with that effortless posture that Mrs. Twainsbury had never managed to inculcate completely in her daughter. Camilla did her best, but when she was tired, her back would touch the back of a chair. She felt that Lady LaCorte could never unbend so far.

Whatever hair she had was stuffed out of sight under a black cap with the merest hint of lavender frill. She must have been very pretty once. Camilla could see that the lines of her face were very good. But the whole expression was so taut with some emotion that she could not guess that Lady LaCorte looked older than her years. Perhaps her widowhood was enough explanation.

For that reason, Camilla fought her instinctive wish to be equally cold in reply. Pride wouldn't help her now; while Nanny Mallow was incapacitated, she herself really had nowhere else to go. She must remain at the Manor on sufferance. She would bite her tongue if necessary and make herself useful.

Inside the room, Sir Philip swung her down to stand barefoot on the hearth rug. "Here, now," he said. "That's not much of a fire." Going down onto one knee, he groped for the poker. "I'll soon have this more lively."

Lady LaCorte lit the candles. "You have baggage, I presume."

"It's at the inn in the village."

"Indeed? I shall lend you some of my things from last year." The offer was coldly made, but Camilla accepted eagerly.

"I should be glad to see the last of this dress for

a while." She turned toward the fire, putting out her hands to the cheerful blaze, smiling thanks to Sir Philip.

He sat back on his heels, the firelight calling forth the deeper highlights in his hair. "Nothing like plenty of wood for the fire. Traipsing around in all this snow makes one appreciate the smaller luxuries."

"I certainly appreciated the ones your cook offered. She was kindness itself. But I must ask: where did she learn to make such wonderful hot chocolate?"

"It's my mother's receipt, handed down from the sixteenth century," Lady LaCorte said. "A family secret."

"A luxury, indeed, even a treasure, my lady," Camilla said. "You should never divulge it to a soul."

"I won't. Except to my children."

"I imagine they adore it." Perhaps her children were the subject that warmed her heart. Certainly the mention of them seemed to soften her hard dislike.

Sir Philip rose to his feet. Letting his hand rest for an instant on her shoulder, he looked with friendliness into her eyes. "I'll leave you to make your arrangements with Beulah. We're not very formal here, but dinner is usually served at approximately half-past six. Don't feel you must come down if you'd rather not."

"It will be no trouble to bring you a tray," Lady LaCorte said in a tone which contradicted her own statement. "Mrs. Mallow will be having one, I'm sure."

"May I answer later?" Camilla said. "I'm not really tired now, but it has been a long day."

Once again, Sir Philip flicked an eyelid. Camilla wasn't quite sure that a wink was proper between

an unmarried gentleman and a spinster, but somehow this little gesture left her feeling more confident. Though the rest of the household confused
her, Sir Philip seemed relatively uncomplicated, a
true gentleman. She was sorry to see him leave,
though it certainly would not have been proper
for him to stay. But his going left her alone with
Lady LaCorte.

CHAPTER FIVE

Lady LaCorte's anger was cold. Her charity was colder still. But the dress and stockings she brought were warm. She laid the things out on the bed. "There is a nightdress there as well," she said, never looking directly at Camilla. "I'm sure you must be tired after your strenuous exertions."

"It wouldn't have been so hard but for the snow."

"A woman must be prepared for difficulties when she sets herself a task," Lady LaCorte said, sounding very much like Camilla's mother.

"I suppose you are right. Especially when the task is so urgent. It seems, though, that emergencies happen when the elements are against one. Otherwise, they'd hardly be emergencies, would they?"

"I don't follow you."

"Well," Camilla said, wishing she'd not begun. "If the weather were ideal, someone would have come to Nanny Mallow's aid sooner, and there wouldn't have been an emergency. Or at least not so great a one. Tinarose said she sometimes goes to Nanny Mallow's, when you permit it."

"Mrs. Mallow is an ignorant old woman. Only fools and children heed her."

"She was my mother's nurse," Camilla said. "Mother still takes her advice, and I can assure you, Lady LaCorte, she is neither a child nor a fool."

"Ah, yes," she said as if reminded of something she'd meant to say. "Your family. You are not related to anyone living here in Bishop's Halt, are you?"

"I have little family, Lady LaCorte. A mother and a sister only."

"Your father is deceased?"

Camilla nodded.

"Who was he?"

She didn't like to be questioned in such a way, but she felt Lady LaCorte had the right to do so. After all, she could be anyone, a fast woman or a fallen angel, and Lady LaCorte needs must think of her daughters. Camilla only hoped Lady LaCorte would be satisfied with her answers.

"His father was the Earl of Pentrithe, in Scotland. Under attainder, I'm afraid, after the '45."

"Rebels?" Lady LaCorte gave her a glance at that, even more scornful than her previous unwillingness to look at her.

"Not my father. He wasn't born until long after. But his father knew about it. Father said he'd heard his father talk about the men coming to the muster, barefooted and dirty, but the finest fighting men in the world. Of course, my grandfather was only a sixteen-year-old boy at the time."

"You're Scots, then," she said as if that explained everything.

"I suppose one could say that. I've never been there. My father grew up in France."

"French?" Lady LaCorte seemed even more horrified by this than by the notion of rebellion, odd in light of her name.

"Oh, he came back to England before the Revolution. It was quite safe after so long. His older brother had paid to have the title reinstated by then. It's a pity he has no male heirs." She remembered too late that this might be a tender subject for the highly pregnant lady before her.

"So you are the daughter of the second son of an earl," Lady LaCorte summed up, her tone even more barbed. "Who is your mother, then? The natural daughter of the Empress of China?"

"No, the legitimate daughter of a general who thought that marrying my father would be one long romantic story. I don't know how she feels about it now. It always seemed romantic to me. They traveled a great deal. My sister was born in Portsmouth, and I was born in York, which only goes to prove—"

"What? What does it prove?"

"That my father had wandering feet, I suppose. Until his death, we never lived two years in the same town."

"How peculiar."

"Yes, I suppose so. But I loved it. Always something new to see, strange people to meet, neverwalked byways waiting for exploration. . . ." As she spoke, she recalled her father saying something very much like this once as she rode beside him on the roof of a carriage. She couldn't have been more than six or eight. She remembered that Linny, never a good traveler, had been sick and had ridden inside with Mother. She'd been more than glad to get out in the fresh air.

"Difficult for your mother, however. When I came to the Manor—" She stopped suddenly as if remembering that she was speaking to a stranger not deserving of confidence.

"I suppose it must have been. Mother doesn't talk much about such things."

"Where is she now? Staying in the village, perhaps?"

"No," Camilla said, now thoroughly lost. "She's traveling to give aid to my sister, who finds herself in the same condition as you yourself, ma'am."

The white hand, decorated only with the thinnest of golden wedding bands, lifted to smooth unconsciously over the mound of her abdomen. "Is she married?"

Camilla drew herself up, giving Lady LaCorte a glance in which anger was mixed with disappointment. She'd hoped for better of a woman of greater age and rank than herself. "Of course. Married three years or more to John Armistead of Leeds, a rising attorney of the city. I take leave to tell you that your insinuation is insulting, ma'am, not only to my mother and my sister, but to myself."

"Tempestuous creature, aren't you?" her ladyship said, seeming pleased rather than angered by Camilla's outburst. For the first time, she looked fully into her eyes. "You may be the thoroughly nice girl you seem, or you may prove a conniver. Perhaps you are no more than as impetuous as my own girls. Whatever the reason you have come to the Manor, I hope you'll be comfortable here until you find other accommodation. Dinner has been moved back until seven o'clock. Join us if you wish."

Lady LaCorte swept out of the room in her heavy gleamless dress. Even her shoes and stockings, glimpsed under her very long dress as she lifted the hem, were black as the bottom of a well.

Camilla sank down on the bed, another trespass

against her mother's sacred rules. She pursed her lips and blew hard, just evading a whistle. Twice, at least, Camilla had heard in Lady LaCorte's voice such an air of miserable despair that she'd forgiven her on the spot for her sharpness. But it seemed as though the older woman had wanted to make her disdain very clear as almost every word she'd said, by content or by tone, had been reviling and rude. Camilla could not begin to explain it. Unfortunately, Lady LaCorte had been too harsh to permit Camilla to indulge in any of the whys that crowded her mouth.

Merridew brought up the tub, grumbling away. Mavis and another younger girl, who never opened her lips or looked her way, brought up the cans of hot water, making several trips.

Clean, warm and dry, Camilla didn't trouble anyone to help her dress. Her hair was not so bad as she feared. The dress Lady LaCorte had lent her was simple in design, with a crossover front that meant all the ties and fastenings were within Camilla's reach. Of a lightweight green wool, embroidered on bodice and down the seams with white-work leaves and flowers, it was too old for her. The high starched ruffle at the neck forced her to keep her head up while the sleeves tumbling to her knuckles made her wonder if the dining room was very drafty.

She paused in Nanny Mallow's chamber for an instant. Nanny was asleep, and Mrs. Duke would brook not the slightest chance of waking her. She all but pushed Camilla out of the room by continuing to advance, hissing all the while in a hoarse whisper, until Camilla had either to become nose-to-nose with her or back away. She chose discretion.

"It's bad enough that doctor had to come in,

disturbing her just when she'd nodded off, without you doing the same, miss. All she needs now is a mite of sleep, and that she'll have or my name's not Portia Duke."

"Is it?" Camilla asked, finding it hard to believe. But no one was responsible for their name, only what it stood for. "How pretty," she added quickly.

"M'father was fond of a word of poetry in the evenings, poor man."

" 'The quality of mercy is not strained,' " Camilla began.

"That's right." Mrs. Duke seemed puzzled that anyone besides her father should know it. "Mortal fond of poems and such like. Don't know where he took a taste for such stuff, him being no better than a coachman." She sniffed. "No sense to it, mostly."

"Your father must have been a remarkable man."

"He was a good provider. My mother says you can't expect more from a man than that."

"My mother says the same thing," Camilla noted. Of course, Mrs. Twainsbury masked her meaning rather more than Mrs. Duke's mother. She talked about the duty a girl owed to her family not to marry beneath herself. Though the daughter of a general might equal the second son of an earl, Camilla had always wondered secretly if her mother had felt herself to have married up or down on the social scale.

Mrs. Duke seemed suddenly to remember that she disliked Camilla. All the same, she grudgingly promised to offer her good wishes to Nanny Mallow, should she awaken. Then she slipped back into the sickroom and shut the door quietly but firmly.

At almost the same instant, Camilla heard a door open on the floor above. She frankly listened, hoping for some clue to her reception at the Manor.

Though she had not expected to be received with open arms and a military band playing "See the Conquering Hero," the cool unfriendliness of the inhabitants, even if tempered by charity, was starting to make her doubt herself. Was her breath somehow offensive? Did she remind them all of some acquaintance better forgot?

A quite young and rather loud voice sounded from above. "But I don't see why you should be allowed to eat with the grown-ups while we have to take our tea up here."

"It's not fair," another voice chimed in, younger, yet somehow deeper. "You've got your cameo on. We're not even allowed to look at ours."

"That's because you're children," Tinarose said. Camilla could imagine the young girl's nose tilted in the air. "A lady like me needs a little touch of jewelry to set me apart from the governesses and companions." Her sisters greeted this attempt at pretension with hoots of laughter, then a scream as a sudden swift thud of a charge took place. Lighter feet skipped away over Camilla's head.

Camilla dipped two fingers into the high lace collar that scratched so abominably at her neck. She caught hold of and dragged out her gold locket on a thin chain. With a wry smile, she laid it to repose on her bosom. It had been made on the Continent and was said to be quite fine. She, at least, would not be relegated to the status of governess or lady's companion, two fates which she prayed she need never attempt.

She waited patiently on the landing until Tinarose stopped chasing after her sisters. When Tinarose caught sight of her as she came down a level, her steps grew slower and more deliberate on the uncarpeted stairs to the third floor.

"Are you lost?" she asked, the tone friendly.

"I don't know the way to the dining room."

"Oh, my uncle isn't there."

"I wasn't looking for him. Your mother said I might join the family for dinner if I didn't feel like taking a tray in my room. I would like company, so here I am."

"You saw Mother?"

"Yes. She lent me a few things for the night."

Tinarose nodded as if Camilla had confirmed something for her. "I thought I recognized the dress."

"It's very pretty. I'm very grateful to her."

"Mother doesn't like it. Of course, she couldn't wear it anyway. Not now."

"I was sorry to hear of your father's death," Camilla said with compassion. "He must have been a most gallant officer."

"He was," Tinarose said, gazing off into the distant view afforded by the upper-landing window. "Two of his crew nearly drowned trying to save him." Then the girl turned her head and gave Camilla a slight, sweet smile. "Come on. I'll show you where the drawing room is. We always meet there first."

As they went down together, Camilla became aware of a kind of suppressed excitement simmering in the girl beside her. Her cheeks held a tinge of color, and her eyes were bright. She'd also obviously taken some extra pains with her abundant dark hair, creating several large springing curls at either side of her head. It was becoming to her but far too elaborate for a quiet family party. Camilla wished she knew Tinarose a little better so that she might have dropped a gentle hint.

"I am intrigued, Miss LaCorte, by your name. Tinarose. Does it have some significance?"

"I was named for both my grandmothers," she

said with a smile that indicated she'd often been asked. "My father was afraid that one name or the other would drop away, so he linked them into one so that neither would have preference."

"A very fair decision."

"What about you?"

"Oh, I was named for some Roman heroine. Or perhaps she wasn't Roman. All I recall is that she ran so lightly that she could run over a field of growing crops without bending a stalk. Sir Philip would probably know more."

"Does your mother admire that kind of person?"

"Doesn't everyone?" Camilla saw the girl having trouble answering this rhetorical question. "Now, my sister has a charming name. Linnet. Named for the birds that sang during my parents' honeymoon."

"How romantic," Tinarose said, turning toward her. "Is your sister older or younger?"

"Older, by two years."

"Oh."

She sounded so disappointed that Camilla laughed. "Why, did you want her to be younger?"

"No, it's only . . . Well, I have two sisters, both younger than I. They're the bane of my life, they tease me so. I thought if you were in the same case, you could offer me some advice."

"You're fond of them?"

"They can be such dears," Tinarose conceded. "But I'm sixteen and Nelly is ten and Grace is only six. They don't understand what it is to be a woman."

Camilla, hardly twenty-one herself, did not smile at the mingled pride and resignation in Tinarose's voice. She had not yet entirely outgrown the feeling that no one could understand her. "It's difficult," she said. "I remember my sister at your age. I thought she was impossible. She'd been a darling before that; we shared so much since there was only the two of us. It's hard to watch a beloved sister go through the door to womanhood, leaving you behind."

"Are you close again now?"

Camilla shook her head. "Not yet. But I hope to be again, once I catch up to her. She's married now. I'm only here because my mother has gone to be with her through her first confinement."

Tinarose's eyes grew wide. "Oh, how you must miss being with her!"

"Yes, yes, I do. But my mother thought it wisest for me not to go just now." Camilla realized that they'd been standing together for some few minutes outside a pair of closed double doors. "Is this the drawing room?" she asked.

Tinarose repressed a giggle. "Yes, it is. Oh, do I . . . Is my hair all right?"

"Charming," Camilla said. "I meant to compliment you upon it." There was no point in lessening the girl's confidence by saying anything less than positive about the confection now. "And what a lovely cameo."

Tinarose touched the carved red and white piece at her throat. The profile was that of a young man, his hair dressed in the Roman fashion now aped by *au courant* gentlemen, his cheeks chiseled and firm chin held high. "My father brought us each one," she said, "I think he bought them in Naples."

"It's sardonyx, isn't it?"

"Yes, but how did you know? Most people think it's made of carnelian." Tinarose opened the doors.

"I read a great deal," Camilla said and noticed

that everyone in the drawing room had turned at their entrance and therefore, they'd all heard her.

"I'm glad to hear it," Sir Philip said, putting down his glass. "I tell my nieces that knowledge becomes a woman just as much as her fair face."

Camilla shook hands with him. "That looks a little as if you were hoping for the best of both worlds, Sir Philip."

"And why not? I always take the best that I am offered. Sherry?"

"Thank you."

He led her to a corner of one of the straw yellow sofas that framed the room. The whole of the drawing room was decorated in warm tones of amber, a springlike contrast to the bitterness of the season. A large fire burned in the white marble fireplace not far from the sofas, but the heat was tempered by two hand-painted fire screens. She admired the pattern while Sir Philip brought her a glass.

"Miss Twainsbury, may I present Dr. Evelyn March?"

Camilla had already noticed him. No woman alive could have failed to notice him. In profile, he might have posed for Tinarose's cameo head. But this Roman figure was alive, the black coat and white stock of the medical man encasing his broad shoulders and strong neck, the beautifully molded mouth smiling as he shook hands. So good looking a man must cause many maidenly hearts to flutter. She wondered how many of his female patients were truly ill, then reproved herself for the cattiness of the idea.

"A pleasure to meet you, Miss Twainsbury. Nanny Mallow cannot sing your praises enough."

"It is she who was brave," Camilla said, finding

her voice. "I faced nothing worse than a little chill and some inconvenience. I cannot bear to think what she must have suffered before my appearance on the scene."

"We must thank Providence that she only wrenched her knee. These elderly ladies can be surprisingly fragile."

"And surprisingly resilient, too," Sir Philip said. "I've seen them carry half their households on their backs and still make supper for a village."

"Where was that, Uncle Philip?" Tinarose asked.

"Greece. Pennsylvania. St. Kitts. It's the same story the world over."

"I had no notion you were so widely traveled, Sir Philip," Camilla said.

Tinarose answered for him. "Oh, yes. Uncle Philip has been *everywhere.*"

"Not quite everywhere. But it's a very interesting place, our world. I think it behooves a man to see as much of it as he can. My brother preferred to see it from the deck of a ship, but I always liked tramping around on my own two feet."

"Better your own two feet than on a horse's four," Dr. March said, giving Philip a rueful glance.

"You did very well," he answered. "The journey home will be easier yet." The doctor gave a little groan.

"Isn't Dr. March staying here?" Tinarose asked. Camilla glanced at her curiously. Her tone was a trifle too artless to be true. She felt that Tinarose not only knew the doctor would be staying, but she was more than a little pleased by the notion.

This undercurrent of feeling seemed to go unnoticed by the gentlemen.

"I'm afraid I cannot, Miss LaCorte. My father is unwell. I must return tonight."

Sir Philip offered Camilla a glass of sherry. Since

his guest could not dress for dinner, he had not done so either, merely changing his coat from the rough brown fustian he'd worn during the day to a more civilized blue superfine. His cravat was more *à la mode* than his other, carelessly knotted, one. He, like his niece, had evidently taken some care to arrange his dark hair, since the tracks of the comb were still visible in the dampened strands.

Though not as jaw-droppingly handsome as the doctor, he looked even more like someone she'd like to know well than the man she'd met in the coach. Then, he'd been someone to ignore or even to snub in accordance with her mother's imperatives. Now, since fate or Providence had thrown them into acquaintanceship, she wished to further it.

Not merely, she told herself, because he was both attractive and pleasantly spoken, but because he'd seen things that she wished to see, had been places that she would like to go, and, undoubtedly, had experienced many adventures that would thrill her as well. Since it was exceedingly unlikely that she'd have any future chance to leave her mother, let alone England, Camilla thought that achieving these ambitions secondhand would be better than not achieving them at all.

Seeing that Dr. March had gone on to regale Tinarose with the tale of his attempts to ride, Camilla smiled encouragingly at Sir Philip. "You must have enjoyed your opportunities to travel, sir. Is it only restiveness that has taken you to these far corners of the world? Or do you have some end in view?"

"I wish I could fascinate you with my noble reasons for undertaking my journeys," he said, seating himself beside her. "My brother had the excuse of his duty. I, on the other hand, had only what the

Germans call *wanderlust*. I simply set out one morning from this front door and walked away."

"Just like that?"

He chuckled. "There was some little preparation involved, of course. I didn't run down the drive without so much as a florin or a clean shirt. Perhaps next time I shall try that."

"What did your parents think of your leaving home? How old were you?" She stopped. "I don't mean to be inquisitive."

"Why not? If you don't ask questions, how will you learn?"

"Socrates?"

"Perhaps. It only makes sense, but I can't prove it." He observed her in silence for a moment. "You know Socrates?"

"Not firsthand. Very little of my knowledge comes firsthand. I don't read Greek or Latin, so I only know the ancient philosophers through what others have written about them. Several of my friends at home know them well, however."

"Female friends?" he asked.

Camilla shook her head slightly. "Several gentlemen of my neighborhood have formed the habit of stopping by several times a month at my mother's house. They discuss lofty subjects."

"Sounds like the Royal Society."

"With this exception—women are not even permitted to listen at the Royal Society."

"Nor to speak?" He raised one eyebrow loftily.

Camilla was forced to laugh. "Not very often, perhaps. They would be distressed to discover how little of their discourse I . . . I understand."

"Now, why do I believe," he began, sitting back against the cushion, "that you intended to say not how little you understand but how little you agree with them."

"Perhaps, but it isn't very grammatical or polite to say so." Camilla turned her face toward Dr. March and Tinarose. Sir Philip saw entirely too much with his parti-colored eyes.

"You say these young men come to your mother's house several times a month. Why? Haven't they any of their own to go to?"

"Several."

"Yet they come to your mother's house. There must be some powerful inducement there."

"Oh, there is," she said, turning her gaze upon him again. She smiled secretly to see him taken aback and was pleased to know that he had already a high enough opinion of her demureness to be surprised by her seeming immodesty. She let him hang upon his regret for a moment. "My mother bakes the most delicious *beignet de pommes* on earth. Not even you, widely traveled though you are, have ever tasted better."

"Can you make them?"

"I haven't her lightness of touch with the pastry."

"I think your touch is sufficiently light for anything."

The look that passed between them then was not measurable in anything but heartbeats, the oldest form of timekeeping and the most accurate when it came to gauging feelings. Sir Philip's eyes were telling her that the physical admiration he'd known in the coach had already deepened into an acknowledgment of pleasure in her company and conversation. Camilla could not prevent a warmer feeling blossoming in her own breast. She felt that she'd met a friend.

For all that, a chilly feeling arose with the consciousness that she had already cracked, if not broken, several of her mother's most dearly held and

most often reiterated rules. Perhaps it was "fast" to
be too friendly even when every feeling encouraged her to ripen this friendship. Therefore, it was
Camilla who looked away first.

Then Lady LaCorte came in, and the instant
blackening of her face when she saw Sir Philip and
Camilla *tête-à-tête* informed Camilla that she'd made
an enemy.

CHAPTER SIX

At dinner, Camilla saw several servants she'd not realized the manor house possessed. There was a frigidly correct butler whose name seemed, however unlikely, to be Samson. Mavis did not serve, but an older maid whose quiet urging to "take another chop, do," proclaimed her to be one of Mrs. Duke's children.

Since the numbers were uneven and they only used half the large table, Camilla sat alone on one side, while Sir Philip and Lady LaCorte bracketed her at the head and foot. Tinarose sat next to the doctor on the other side.

In the golden glow of the many-branched candelabra, Dr. March glowed like a highly polished bronze statue. His thoughts and words were those of a man of science while his appetite was that of a young man who'd taken unaccustomed exercise in winter.

"I have been meaning to learn to ride, but there never seemed to be enough time now that I'm living here. There certainly was no time while I was training."

"Of course, you lived in town then, didn't you?" Tinarose said, making excuses.

"Edinburgh," he said. "They have horses there, but they also have very hard streets."

"Hard streets?"

"You know. Cobblestones and the like. I couldn't see learning to ride there. All the falling off."

"You should learn to ride while the snow is still thick upon the ground. It will be safer for you."

"I found it no less distressing," he said, glancing with a half laugh at Sir Philip.

"Oh, come. It was only the once, and you landed in a large snowbank. Believe me, I didn't get off nearly so gently when I learned. It was during the longest drought in years. The ground was like a sheet of iron. As I remember well," he added with a reminiscent grimace.

"Yes, but how old were you?"

"Six, I think. It was the year before I went to school."

"Ah," the doctor said. Turning to Tinarose, he leaned toward her confidentially. "The young, Miss LaCorte, being more flexible may take a toss without harm. We who are older cannot so easily recoup from such a shock."

At first, Tinarose's eyes flickered in pained surprise when he seemed to refer to her as young. But the latter half of his comment, grouping her in the "older" category with him, made her smile hopefully and nod her complete agreement.

Camilla glanced at the black and silent figure at the end of the table. Lady LaCorte showed animation only whenever Sir Philip spoke to Camilla. Her own daughter's lively interest in the doctor seemed to escape her notice.

As a good guest, Camilla tried to divide her attention evenly between her hostess and her host. She attempted to develop topics of interest to whichever of them she was speaking. Yet even while discussing the virulent weather with Sir Philip and praising the excellence of the dinner to Lady LaCorte, Camilla's mind busied itself with the mystery of the Manor. It could not be that Lady LaCorte had transferred her affections so quickly from her husband to her brother-in-law.

Not because such matters were beyond the scope of the human heart in even less time than the length of Lady LaCorte's widowhood, but she gave no sign of even being fond of Sir Philip. She lapsed into silence more often than she spoke, staring off at the dark corners of the room where the candle-light could not quite reach.

So if it was not love and its accompanying jealousy that plagued Lady LaCorte, what was the fount of her dislike for Camilla? Mere natural antipathy? The whim of a pregnant woman? All well and good, but what about the others? Surely the servants could not be so completely under her sway that they'd dislike someone on her orders?

Having lived with her mother for her entire life with often no more service than that offered by one maid who obliged by the day and spent the nights at her parents' farm, Camilla had not enough experience of master-servant relationships to know how far a mistress's influence might extend. But considering that the servants had disliked her long before Lady LaCorte could have heard of her presence, Camilla was still confused. She resolved to watch and wait.

"You said you like to read, Miss Twainsbury," Dr. March said. "What is your field of study?"

"No field, sir, or all of them."

"Ah, novels," the doctor said, looking wise or, at any rate, arch. "A young woman's *Thousand and One Nights.*"

"My mother does not approve of novels."

A slight sound of malicious humor came from Lady LaCorte's end of the table. "Wise creature, your mother. I don't approve of them either. They pretend to be moral works, but they excite unnatural passions in young persons. Better to read a morally improving work."

Camilla caught the whisper of an undercurrent that she did not understand. Something in Sir Philip's expression, seen uncertainly in the glow of the flickering candles, made her believe his sister-in-law was somehow twitting him.

"At least so my mother believes," Camilla said. "So to please her, I read a great deal of history."

"History?" Tinarose so far forgot herself as to groan.

"That sounds safe enough," young Dr. March pronounced.

Sir Philip nodded, encouraging her to go on.

"Is it any safer than novels?" she asked rhetorically. "I haven't found it to be so. I took up history because my mother forbade me to read novels. Yet what did I find in history but the same passions that make novels so exciting."

"But it's all so dry," Tinarose said. "Our governess, Miss Grayle, makes us read all the most dreary things. Dates and battles and tonnage moved from the principle ports."

"You have to look past that," her uncle said. "That's only a kind of fog history wraps herself in. Once you make an effort to see more clearly, history begins to fascinate. Think of all the human passions found in history. Violence, ambition, a kind of lust that sends men mad at times. Not to mention arranged marriages, murders, and mysteries. Who killed the Princes in the Tower? Why was Darnley murdered . . . or was it a royal execution? Was Lucrezia Borgia truly as black as she is painted?"

Camilla laughed and added her own set of fascinations. "Why did Shakespeare leave Stratford? Is the Dauphin still alive somewhere? And as for our own times—was Byng guilty? How did Napoleon escape from Elba?"

"There's not much doubt about Byng," Dr. March said. "But I've always wondered about Dr. Dee. And the Comte Saint-Germain. Were they charlatans? Or did they know things about the universe the rest of us can hardly guess."

Sir Philip seemed to have no doubts. "Definitely charlatans, if the kings of their kind," he said. "But how did they work their magic? They easily persuaded kings and queens that they had gifts of prophecy and could turn base metal into shining gold."

"It may be revolutionary to say it," Camilla said, "but I'm not sure royalty is known for their intellectual gifts."

Even Lady LaCorte chuckled while the gentlemen laughed. Only Tinarose looked shocked and that only slightly. "You *have* studied history," Sir Philip said, chuckling.

When at home, through some excess of courage, she'd been tempted into making a comment during a philosophical discussion, her visitors would always agree with her. It left her feeling as if her comments were not worthy of argument. Eventually, on her mother's advice, she'd learned to sit in silence, letting even the most crashing fallacies pass over her head. Mrs. Twainsbury was of the firm opinion that intellectual pursuits were not within a woman's province and that no sensible man would wish them to become so.

Certainly she never would have dared to comment in such a way that could be considered openly seditious. Yet among these strangers, she felt not only secure enough to do so, but encouraged to participate to the height of her abilities.

"I make exceptions," Camilla said. "Queen Elizabeth certainly had intellectual gifts."

"Greater than Mary, Queen of Scots, anyway," Sir Philip said. "I know women tend to make her story out to be romantic—"

"Not just women." Even more daring, Camilla interrupted. "My father thought she was beyond reproach. I always felt she was a silly creature. Why didn't she learn to be more moderate in her actions instead of continually stirring up trouble for herself?"

The doctor nodded wisely. "That's a question I can apply to half a dozen people I know very well."

"Which one is Mary, Queen of Scots?" Tinarose asked, with a shy glance at her mother. "There've been so many Marys."

The doctor began to explain the delicate relationship between Queen Elizabeth and her cousin, the once-Queen of France and mother of the man who united England and Scotland. Camilla somehow believed that Tinarose would not forget this history lesson anytime soon. She had not yet met the LaCorte's governess, but the woman could not possibly compete with the words of a terribly attractive man.

When Samson took a moment of his mistress's time to hold her in whispered conversation, Camilla turned to Sir Philip. "I hope I did not speak out of turn just now."

"Is there such a thing? After all, this isn't Almack's. Just a simple country dinner."

"Be that as it may, I did interrupt you. Also, my mother does not like me to speak in company. She says it is unbecoming in the young to speak in the presence of those older and wiser."

"She presumes wisdom: I don't." His voice was rather a growl. Camilla drew back, giving him a sideways glance, doubtfully. "I beg your pardon," he said, noticing her reaction. "Only some people achieve wisdom with years. Many others remain just as filled with folly, pride, and self-importance as any green youngster."

"Would you say that you are like that?"

"I hope not."

"Then, I should indeed apologize for interrupting you."

"That puts us back where we began."

"Not at all. Before I apologized as a matter of form, in deference to your greater age and position. Now that you have proved yourself worthy of my respect, I apologize without reserve. Wholeheartedly, in fact."

Though he smiled at her wit, she saw something of displeasure in his eyes. "I'm not that old," he said. "You make me sound like a hoary-bearded grandfather, complete with bad leg and ear trumpet. I'm not even thirty, not until April. Though to someone as young as yourself—"

"I'm twenty-one," she said, interrupting again. Realizing she'd risen to his bait, she the more willingly gave her attention to Dr. March when he claimed his turn to speak to Sir Philip.

"I was just telling Miss LaCorte about that cold winter we spent in Paris."

"Yes, I remember your hospitality very well. You

kindly gave me the bed while you slept rolled up in two blankets on the sofa. Kindness itself," he added. "Until the roof started to leak. Ice-cold water. But it was colder by far in Badajoz, or so you told me."

"Oh, were you there during the siege?" Tinarose asked.

"Briefly," the doctor said. "But I was telling you about Paris. There I was, one of about fourteen doctors holed up in this tumble-down town house, assured by *la concierge* that her palace had housed doctors since the fourteenth century, and judging by the beds, I believed her."

"Whatever were you doing in Paris, Dr. March?" Camilla asked, fascinated.

"A group of us were pressed into service by the army directly after leaving school. I knew it would be my only chance to see something of the world, and as my father made no objection, I went. After a little service in the south—"

"A little?" Sir Philip cried. "You were in that hell-hole for six years, man! Tell her about Badajoz and Madrid."

Camilla couldn't help but be aware of the under-currents at the table. Sir Philip, for whatever reason, seemed to want to turn his friend's reminiscences into some other channel. The doctor, whether through having taken too much wine or just through a natural perversity, seemed intent on embarrass-ing his friend with his story.

"I want to talk about Paris," Dr. March insisted. "So there I was, attached now in some convoluted fashion to Old Hookey's Embassy to Louis, coming back to this dismal flat from a hard day's service."

"To wounded soldiers?" Tinarose asked, leaning forward with an elbow on the table.

"No, to some fat major's wife who'd caught a bad cold just before some *soiree* or other. So imag-

ine me, my coat flapping in the chill breeze blowing between the avenues, looking forward to a cut
off the roast and a bottle of bad red wine, stumbling over a corpse on my very doorstep."

"Dr. March!" Lady LaCorte said sharply. "We are
at table, sir."

But he only turned his handsome, smiling face
in her direction. "Don't be alarmed. He wasn't
quite dead. I rolled the body over and found, grin-
ning up at me, my old friend from home. Rather a
mess, he was, too. You see . . ."

"Not a tale for the ladies, old chap," Sir Philip
said hastily, covering the doctor's voice with his
own.

But Dr. March simply repeated his remarks.
"He'd been stabbed in the back."

Everyone at the table, even the servants, stared
more or less openly at Sir Philip. He only shook his
head. "Coffee, I think, Samson."

"Stabbed? Uncle Philip?" Tinarose looked at her
uncle as if she'd never seen him before. "How . . . I
mean, who did it?"

Sir Philip said nothing, turning his wineglass,
seemingly absorbed in the tawny depths.

"He spun me some tale of an accident. Needless
to say, I didn't believe a word of it and still don't. I
patched him up, of course, and offered him a bed
for the night. I swear I never thought about the roof
leaking. He spent a few days with me and then dis-
appeared. In another month, we all left Paris to accompany the Duke to Vienna."

"I didn't 'disappear,'" Sir Philip said, speaking
at last. "I simply arrived in Vienna before you. We
met there, and I can't say it was any warmer there
than in Paris, except that waltzing is excellent exercise. Do you remember the Countess von
Steich's evening parties?"

At last the doctor let himself be led down another conversational path. Why had he told that story about Paris? She glanced at Sir Philip, now reminding the doctor of some chance-met young woman, and wondered, as perhaps she was meant to, about him and his past.

Samson returned and had another word in her ladyship's ear. Camilla reluctantly gave her attention to Lady LaCorte when she tapped her knife against her crystal goblet.

"As our friends know, we have entertained but little since news came of my husband's death." Her voice sank for a moment; then she rallied. "Nevertheless, there are certain customs of the country that must be observed, more especially at this time of the year."

Camilla had seen Tinarose look down into her lap and close her eyes at the mention of her father. But then she looked up and brightened at the hopeful trend of her mother's words.

"Though it lacks some hours until midnight and the arrival of Stir-up Sunday, Mrs. Lamsard in the kitchen and Mr. Samson have persuaded me to stretch a point so that our guests might participate. Tinarose, will you ask Miss Grayle to bring down your sisters?"

"Yes, Mother. They'll be so happy."

The kitchen looked very different from Camilla's first visit there. Someone had hung ribbon-tied swatches of dried herbs and flowers from the ceiling beams, giving the whole room the mysterious, exciting smell of an apothecary's shop. The cold glow of moonlight on snow that came through the high windows met the golden gleams of candles that burned lavishly on tabletop and counter, on windowsill and barrel.

Camilla heard whispering and perceived in the shadows of the large room that others had come for the ceremony. She felt her own strangeness. Everyone belonged to the Manor in some way, whether they served it in house or field, or lived under its roof and cared for it. For she'd known from her first conscious step in this house that it was well loved.

When she hesitated on the doorstep, knowing herself to be an outsider, Dr. March was behind her. "Is something wrong?"

"No, I . . . What is Stir-up Sunday?"

The doctor looked at her with surprise. "You don't know?"

"No, sir."

"And you do live in England?"

"Not a day's journey from here. Is this custom so universal? I have never heard of it."

The doctor tilted his head to one side in a motion that might have been a shrug. Whatever hilarity had affected him at dinner seemed to have faded. "Usually it is done among the lower classes; servants and so on seem fond of it."

"Perhaps that's why I've not heard of it. We keep only one servant, and she is unusually taciturn. Some weeks she hardly speaks at all."

"You must find the Manor a most remarkable change," he said with a lowered voice. "It's an interesting house, nearly as interesting as the people who live in it. As for the pudding," he said, in a more normal tone, "my father would no more miss stirring the Christmas pudding than he'd refuse to go out on an emergency visit."

"But a doctor isn't of the lower classes."

"Perhaps not in such an enlightened place as you come from, Miss Twainsbury. What is the name of your place of residence?" She told him, and he nodded. "You wouldn't happen to be in need of a doctor's services there?" he asked with his quick smile. "Well, no matter; I can't leave Bishop's Halt while my father needs me." He fell silent.

"And Stir-up Sunday?" Camilla prompted.

"Oh, yes. Pray excuse me. This is the time when every member of the household, oldest to youngest, gives the Christmas pudding three stirrings. Each person is to make three wishes, one of which is certain to come true before next Christmas."

"What will you wish for, Dr. March?"

"The usual sort of thing, I suppose. Riches beyond avarice, long life, and a pair of warm slippers."

"Warm slippers? Among such grand wishes, you wish for warm slippers?"

"I did say that only one wish would come true, didn't I? Wealth and health may come or not, but my housekeeper always makes my father and me warm slippers for Christmas."

"Perhaps if you didn't wish for slippers, one of your other wishes would come true," Camilla said.

He laughed. "I've never been one to take mad risks," he said. "Unlike some I could name."

"You mean Sir Philip? He hardly seems like the reckless sort."

"Didn't you hear what I told you at the table? I don't know what happened in Paris, but I do know that wasn't the only time I found him in mysterious circumstances. I used to know him so well. We were always friends. Lately, though, I feel as if I only know the outer man, this gentle squire pose he's adopted since coming back to the Manor."

"You think he is playacting?" Camilla asked.

"Can a man change so much? He was a wild boy, almost uncontrollable. As a youth, he took mad chances. True, he always came out of them well, barring a broken arm or some such, but I worry. . . ."

"I'm a stranger here, Dr. March," Camilla said, suddenly feeling as if she were being warned to stay away. Perversely, this warning only made her want to explore forbidden territory more closely. "Such things are not my concern."

"No, of course not."

Sir Philip came to them. "Come, come, no conspiracies," he said. "You can't share your wishes, you know. As guests, you must stir first." He took Camilla's hand in his warm clasp and tucked it beneath his arm. "Come along."

They waited, however, until the younger two children came in, shuffling along in matching quilted robes with felt slippers upon their feet. The doctor and Camilla exchanged a glance. "Tell me the joke," Sir Philip whispered in her other ear.

"Nothing important. What happens now?"

"Listen," he said. His breath was warm and fragrant with the wine he'd drunk at dinner. She found herself breathing in a little more deeply, feeling how close he stood beside her.

Camilla had only ever drunk water or sweet cider at meals. She'd found the one glass of rich red wine she'd had, served with a chine of beef and removes of pigeon pie and salmi of woodcock, to be both delicious and drying. She'd had to request a glass of water from Mr. Samson and had been glad, thereafter, to be served the same drinks as Tinarose.

Nevertheless, the single glass of red wine must have done something to disturb her equilibrium.

Why else would she feel this urgent temptation to
lean against Sir Philip, to feel his strong arm come
about her waist in support? She'd been raised to
stand firmly on her own two feet and to know right
from wrong no matter what clever disguises wrong
took on. It must certainly be wrong to wish to rub
her cheek against the smooth wool of his coat like
a cat finding her master. Only the unaccustomed
taste of alcohol could explain this sudden sapping
of her moral fiber. She vowed she'd never take another glass.

As though the entrance of the children was a
signal, from every corner of the room servants stepped forward to stand beside the large, well-scrubbed
table in the center of the room. Camilla saw now
that an enormous bowl stood in the center, ringed
about with garlands of dried flowers. A topiary
tree made of some evergreen plant stood beside
the bowl. The cook, Mrs. Lamsard, stood behind
the bowl, wearing her dazzlingly white apron but
having added what was evidently her very best bonnet.

At her nod, the servants broke into song. Camilla
couldn't quite make out the words, something about
the sun or the Son. She found herself smiling at
Sir Philip as he sang along, tunelessly and all but
inaudibly under his breath. "This is my favorite
part," he said.

Merridew started it. "Suet for Bartholomew," he
said, leaning forward to touch the bowl, and then
turned to the man next to him.

"Sugar for Matthew," he mumbled, several front
teeth missing. He touched the bowl and turned to
a younger woman.

"Raisins for Mark."

"Currants for Luke."

"Crumbs for John."

Camilla looked up at Sir Philip, puzzled.

"There are thirteen ingredients in a good Christmas pudding," he whispered. "One for each Apostle and Christ, too."

"What does Judas get?" she asked softly.

"I don't know. The egg shells, perhaps."

When the reading of the ingredients came to an end, Mrs. Lamsard beckoned Camilla forward. Camilla hesitated, not sure of her place in this ritual. Sir Philip gave her a little push. "Go on."

Coming nearer, she saw that from several branches of the little tree, silver charms hung twinkling. As she watched, Mrs. Lamsard pulled the charms off, one at a time, and dropped them into the bowl. "Wedding ring means marriage," she said, her curiously deep voice rumbling like heat in a chimney. "Button means bachelor. Thimble leaves an old maid. Tuppence is lucky."

She dropped the last charm into the dark brown batter. The semisolid mass accepted it with the sound of a kiss. Mrs. Lamsard picked up a wooden spoon. "Three times you stir, sunwise, and you makes your wishes," she said.

Camilla met the woman's eyes and raised her eyebrows, mouthing, "Sunwise?" With a thick forefinger, Mrs. Lamsard drew a circle showing her the way to go.

Camilla knew just enough not to say her wishes aloud. The memory of childhood games played with her sister came back. One must never ever tell a wish, for that breaks the spell, spilling all the luck out of it so that it will never ever come true.

She had no intention of making a wish. She didn't believe in wishes or dreams. Such things were for children and not always for them. Yet as she pushed the thick wooden spoon through the batter, knowing this was an ancient action carried out through the centuries, she found herself wishing that she might always have the warmth of friends, the nearness of family, and . . . Her gaze lifted for one turn of the spoon, seeking out Sir Philip. Impulsively, she wished for a love that would banish her loneliness, outlast her youth, that would grow warmer and deeper with the passing of the years.

Was that too great a wish for a Christmas pudding? Perhaps she should wish for a packet of needles or a skein of wool, two things she was sure to receive this Christmas as at every Christmas. But she decided as she gave the last stir to be bold, to be, perhaps, foolish and to wish for love.

CHAPTER SEVEN

After Camilla, the doctor stirred the pudding. He looked like a pagan god making preparation for a sacrifice, noble, remote, exalted. Tinarose couldn't take her gaze from his face. For Camilla, who knew he was thinking about slippers, some of the fascination of his remarkable good looks faded.

After the guests came the master of the house. Though he smiled as he took up the wooden spoon, polished like glass from countless Christmas stirrings, when he began his turn, he kept his eyes downward, as if concentrating seriously on his wishes. Camilla wondered what such a man as Sir Philip could desire. He seemed to have everything, a fine home, a close family, status in his community. Perhaps he thought of his late brother. It would explain the pensive expression he wore throughout the superstitious ceremony.

As Lady LaCorte stirred, she kept her left hand flat against her side, as if transferring some of her wishes to her unborn infant. Her daughter looked shyly at the doctor as she took the spoon in her hand. The smaller girls giggled as they passed the spoon from biggest to littlest, then ran laughing back to the governess's skirts. And so it went, among the servants, from old Merridew down to a frightened-looking dairymaid, her fingers red from cold.

Camilla found Sir Philip beside her as the festival ended. "This is where we 'gentry' withdraw and leave them to continue. There'll be cider drunk with cornmeal sprinkled on it and some singing."

"This is a long-standing custom in this house, I take it?"

"Very long. But even older is the custom that when the master leaves, the festivity begins. Once, I could stay quiet in the corner and no one would take notice of me. I was just 'young Mister Philip' then. Now, for all my sins, I am master here and, thus, unwelcome."

He raised his hands, and a silence fell, silence with an undercurrent of laughter and whisperings. "Thank you, Mrs. Lamsard. I'm certain that this year's pudding will be a resounding success." A ragged cheer went up at this. "However, I do make one request. As you all know, everyone should stir the Christmas pudding so that all the household will have good fortune. We have a guest in this house who cannot come down to make her wishes. Therefore, if Mrs. Duke agrees, I ask that the pudding bowl be carried up to Mrs. Mallow's bedside so that she might have her turn."

" 'At's right," seconded Merridew. "Good luck won't stick if someone's left out. I'll carry up the bowl meself."

"That you won't do, Mr. Merridew," Mrs. Lamsard said. Picking up the enormous bowl, she cradled it in the crook of her arm. "I'll do it."

Mrs. Duke tossed off her glass of cider. "I doubt but she'll be awake with all this noise going on. But don't the whole crowd come up. Likely to scare her into fits."

In the end, only Camilla, Sir Philip, and Mrs. Lamsard carried up the bowl. "Oh, is it Stir-up Sunday so soon? I must have lost count of the days," Nanny Mallow said, blinking in the light of the candles.

"No," Mrs. Lamsard said gently. "We be taking care of this today since there's guests in the house. It's not usual, but since everything's prepared . . ."

"Very wise," she said. "Having guests stir the bowl brings more honor on a family than anything. Is it m'turn? Help me sit up, then."

Dr. March came in behind them. Coming to the bed, he picked up Nanny Mallow's wrist and counted silently. "Steady and strong," he pronounced.

Camilla saw that Tinarose had also entered the bedroom. She sat down just inside the entrance, and Camilla realized the girl's affection for the doctor extended to a need to be wherever he was. She wished she knew the girl better so that she might know if this affection was a new thing and whether it was mutual. True, Tinarose was only sixteen, but many of their grandmothers had married that young and done well enough. Yet, honestly, she'd seen no sign that the doctor in any way, shape or form returned the young lady's tender regard.

"I hardly have anything to wish for," Nanny Mallow said, her voice soft and quavering. "I have good friends, a roof over m'head, and all those little things that make m'life so pleasant."

"Why not wish for a speedy return to your strength?" Sir Philip said.

She nodded and took up the spoon, supported by the doctor's good right arm. "I shall not wish for anything for myself," she said. "But I can think of plenty of wishes for the ones I love." Slowly and weakly, she turned the spoon. "Three times toward the sun; then my wishing's done."

"All right, now," Dr. March said soothingly. "Well done. I'm going to mix you a composer," he added, laying her back against the pillows. "Not as good as you make yourself, I'm sure, but I've had good results with it."

Tinarose busied herself with a small decanter and glass that stood on a table by the window. Dr. March brought out a tiny vial from the bag he'd left on the chair. "Now if I could have a glass of . . . Oh, thank you, Miss LaCorte. Very helpful of you."

"Thank you, Doctor," she whispered, her eyes brightened by this scrap of praise. Camilla's heart went out in sympathy to the younger girl. She herself could dimly recall her emotional response to a young curate at Tinarose's age. He'd sung so beautifully on summer evenings that she'd shown a sudden remarkable enthusiasm for the services. By the time he'd been called to his own living, her passion for him had faded. He had, after all, been quite an ordinary young man, and she'd grown wiser since then.

She supposed that all young ladies went through a similar surge of sensibility at about sixteen. She was glad to be through with such feelings now and hoped she might have an opportunity to drop an intrepid word in Tinarose's ear. Though the fate of the unasked-advice giver might be hers, she hated to see someone be hurt when a word from her might lessen the inevitable pain.

Camilla's bed was soft and deep, the covers fluffy, and if a slight odor of must remained in the

room, it was soon banished by the handful of sweet
herbs Mavis had thrown on the fire. The candle,
shaded by a small screen, sent interesting shadows
and lights flickering on the ceiling. After her arduous day, Camilla drifted into sleep like a shallop
setting sail on a calm sea.

Therefore, when she awoke some hours later,
she made every attempt, from flipping and fluff-
ing her pillow to counting sheep, to recover that
blissful state. She failed. Finally, a definite rumble
from her stomach told her why. After two cups of
Mrs. Lamsard's hot cocoa, she had but toyed with
her evening meal. Now, long after any hope of
finding food, she was famished to the backbone.

Sleep being elusive, Camilla began to yearn for
a book. She'd neglected to pack the work she'd
been invested in at home—a fascinating study of
Byzantine political life.

Sitting up and unshading the candle, she
looked around. Though there were shelves in the
room, they were decorated with a series of small
porcelain pieces, less good than the ones she'd
seen downstairs but charming. Someone, perhaps
the late Sir Myron, had been a collector. However,
there was not a book to be seen.

Her better self suggested that she try again to
recapture sleep. But her need for a book seemed
even greater than her empty stomach's demands
for food. Surely, a voice seemed to whisper, in all
this great house there must be a library. True, it
was against every principle to wander about through
a strange house at night, yet she'd already broken
several such rules. This would surely be one that
no one would ever know anything of.

Camilla found her slippers and her wrap laid
out at the end of the bed. Telling herself all the

while that she'd be as quick and quiet as a breeze, Camilla buttoned up to the throat. There were bound to be drafts.

Surprisingly, neither her door nor any of the stairs creaked. The Manor was solidly built. The gilt touches on the picture frames glowed warmly as she descended, her forefinger hooked through the ring of the chamber stick. She held the candle low so that no accident could befall her unbound hair, hanging straight and full from beneath her nightcap.

She knew the dining room was the first door on the left and the drawing room the second. But what rooms were across the hall?

Opening a door, she thrust her candle in and found the light fell on a small round table near a sideboard, glasses and silver set out to be ready for the breakfast. Next to that was a colder room, with blue wallpaper and tasseled curtains. A small gilded harp stood tucked into one corner. Several work cabinets and a table-sized tapestry frame on an easel told her that this must be Lady LaCorte's morning room.

A book, left on a table, drew her farther forward. But, alas, it was the third volume of a novel famous for its bloodcurdling scenes of horror. Camilla left it lying there, admitting to herself that had it been the first volume, she would have been tempted.

Toward the rear of the house, she found a door left its native dark oak, instead of being painted white like the others. Feeling a sudden lift of spirit, she turned the knob boldly and went in.

"Eureka," she whispered as her candle's light played over the gilded spines, warm oxblood, and well-thumbed morocco of filled library shelves. Framed maps and more portraits hung in between tall shelves and over lower ones. She caught a glimpse of Africa in one corner and a long white hand drooping from a lace cuff in another. A thick carpet with a pattern of vines and flowers ran from one end of the room to the other.

It was the most purely "readable" room Camilla had ever seen. There were several comfortable-looking armchairs, a deep leather sofa, and even a window seat between the windows, ideal for curling up for intensive study or dreaming.

Despite the large windows that took up nearly all of the farthest wall, the library was less cold than the other rooms she'd peered into. Camilla walked up close to the nearest shelf and tried to read the titles. Some had none; others only an abbreviation and that in Latin. Still, there must be something she could read here if only she could find it.

Feeling herself to be entirely alone, Camilla was startled by a sudden strange clicking sound, a flicking noise like the striking of flint and steel. At first, she dismissed it, only thinking what a shame that so fine a room should be infested by a deathwatch beetle. But after she turned again to the books, she heard a low growl followed by a whimper.

Walking carefully to keep her candle alight, Camilla moved around the large sofa to find a good dog enjoying the sleep of the just. The sound she'd heard had been Rex's toenails clicking on the marble hearth as he chased a rabbit in his dreams.

Just beyond the dog's back lay a piece of white paper. Camilla bent to pick it up and found that it had been crumpled at least once, then smoothed out again. It was half covered by sprawling handwriting, but her candle did not shed enough light for her to make out any but a few disjointed words.

Looking to see where it had come from, she found a low, double-pedestal table drawn up close to the sofa. More crumpled pages lay scattered over the surface, most clustered close to a portable writing desk. A branch of low-burning candles made a pool of light. The bottle of ink in the holder sat uncapped, a long black pen resting in the ink and casting a strange shadow.

Her curiosity quite unbearable, Camilla tried again to decipher the sheet in her hand.

"I shouldn't bother if I were you. It's terrible."

The sound of a human voice where she'd believed herself alone made Camilla start and gasp. The candle she'd so carefully nurtured dropped from her hand, falling to the tabletop. Instantly, the heavy rag paper began to smolder.

"Oh, dear," Camilla said, reaching out to draw back the candlestick before the disaster increased.

"Let it burn." Sir Philip unfolded himself from the sofa where he'd been lying at full-length in time to grasp her by the wrist. "It's only worthy of being used as a fire starter."

"Be that as it may," Camilla said, twisting free from his slackening hold. "I don't see that it's worth ruining a perfectly good table."

She picked up the candle, but a page already had a line of red glimmering away on one edge, followed by charring, smoke, and destruction.

Sir Philip picked up the page by the farthest end and chucked it into the fireplace near at hand. The last embers of a fire there caught the paper, blackening it into a crumbling mass in seconds. "So shall all my works perish from the earth."

"Your work?" Camilla asked, lightly rubbing the wrist he'd held. Though he'd only exerted his strength for an instant before recollecting himself, she could still feel the imprint of his fingers on her skin.

"I'm a writer," he said glumly. "May God have mercy upon me for my presumption."

"A writer? But how interesting."

"Go on," he said, folding his arms. He had taken off his coat at some point and torn loose his cravat. His dark waistcoat hung unbuttoned around his trim waist, and his shoes were under the table.

"Go on how?" she asked.

"You know. What have I published? Is it under my name? Do I make much money?"

"People don't ask you that, surely."

"Perhaps not directly, but that is the issue they hint at most often. You, though, Miss Twainsbury, are not the kind that hint."

"I hope I'm not the kind who asks impertinent questions about fortune. However, since you insist. . . ." She let the silence build for a breath, then asked, "What have you published, Sir Philip?"

He laughed, and the tension left him. "Two books on my travels, in the Hebrides and America."

"Under what name?"

"Philip Delphos."

She sought in her memory. "I've heard that name, but I don't think I've read any of your books."

"Comparatively few people have," he said with a deprecating smile. "But they were good books."

"Why that name, though? Delphos. What does it mean?"

"It's a town in Greece that everyone thinks is an island, thanks to Shakespeare who got it wrong. The only way to know differently is to go there. Since most people can't travel as they'd like to, I've seen it and described it for them. It's complicated, isn't it?"

"A little."

"Well, I was young and foolish when I chose it.

But it's a good name, short and memorable. Better than 'Bohemia.' "

"Why . . . ?"

"Shakespeare gave Bohemia a seacoast which it lacks."

"You don't like Shakespeare, I take it?"

"Oh, on the contrary. I adore him. I was just lying here cursing his name as a matter of fact."

Camilla felt she'd gone from having a tolerable understanding of Sir Philip LaCorte to wondering if she were not talking to his mysterious twin brother by mistake. "Sir Philip," she said, testingly.

"Yes, Miss Twainsbury?"

She knew she'd regret asking. "Why are you cursing Shakespeare?"

He sighed and stirred the papers on the table with his finger, whether to see if the fire was out or to encourage its embers, she couldn't tell. "I was cursing his blasted gift of invention. Even though his tales are twice-told, he had a gift for making them live again. Since I cannot borrow his gift, I am indulging in a bout of sour grapes."

"Then, this is your new work?" she asked, looking at the litter of papers with more respect.

"Yes and no. It was to be my new work, but I'm surrendering. It's beaten me."

"What is it about? Some other place you have traveled?"

"It's a novel. That's why Beulah was being so severe on the subject while we dined."

Camilla didn't wish to criticize her hostess, however reluctantly Lady LaCorte might have welcomed her. "She doesn't approve of your work?"

"In addition to the fact that no gentleman should wish to work, she doesn't think I'm very good at what I do."

"Yet you have had some success, I think? I should be very interested in reading one of your books."

He bowed graciously. "I gave Myron an inscribed copy of each. I'm sure they're around here somewhere." He walked to the shelves and scanned them. "Here's America and here's the Hebrides. Which one appeals to your taste, Miss Twainsbury?"

"America, please. It is a place that has long held much interest for me. I have an uncle there, I believe."

"Maternal or paternal?"

"Paternal. My father's family scattered to the four winds, rather, after some unfortunate political choices."

"A common fate." He handed her the book.

Camilla seated herself on the sofa and thumbed through the book, bound in olive green cloth with squares of brown leather at the top and bottom of the spine. The title page was beautifully engraved with what looked like the spillings of a cornucopia of native American vegetables and fruits. *"De Novo Republica,* an account of journeying and residence in the bosom of the sometime friendly offspring of Great Britain."

Camilla glanced up at Sir Philip. "You must be very proud. It's a very great accomplishment."

"Not so great. Any fool can write a book; as proof, I offer you any library."

"Still . . . You're the first author I've ever met. Was this your first book?"

"No, I wrote the other one first. This one," he said, tapping the book, "is better."

"I shall take your word for it." Camilla glanced at the rumpled sheets of paper cowering in the pool of light. "What is the trouble with this new one?"

He hitched one shoulder. "The characters, the plot, the setting . . . the author."

"Oh, come. What is the story?"

"Are you certain you want to know?" he asked with one of his sidelong, humorous looks. At her determined nod, he shook his head. "At your request, m'lady. My hero is a young man returning to his ancestral home from whence he'd been unceremoniously booted upon blotting his copybook some years earlier. Oh, I forgot to mention this takes place during the Middle Ages."

"Oh, chivalry," she asked.

"Not at first. My hero is something of a rogue and a wastrel as well as a mercenary. He'll swear loyalty to any man or cause that will pay him. He returns home to find his father dead, his lands heavily taxed by the new landowner, and that his stepmother is the woman he loved before he went away."

"Gracious," Camilla said. "Whatever happens next?"

"At first, he throws his lot in with the new landlord, going in disguise," Sir Philip said, losing much of the speed and flippancy with which he'd begun. "But the suffering of the people he once knew starts to change him. The way the landlord persecutes Genevieve and her patience also begin to soften his heart."

"Doesn't she recognize him?"

"She does, but she's afraid if she reveals his identity, the new landlord will kill him to keep the land."

"Does Genevieve love him?"

"I think so, but of course, they can never marry. The Tables of Kindred and Affinity forbid it."

"Kindred and Affinity? What's that?" Camilla asked with a laugh.

"Rules for marriage so that you don't accidentally marry your father's mother's brother."

"As if I would! Go on; what happens next?"

"He leads a revolt against the cruel landlord in which they both die."

"Wait. He dies?"

"He redeems himself in battle. Of course he dies."

"Must he really? You couldn't make him live?"

"He doesn't have anything to live for. He—"

"Of course he does," Camilla said abruptly. "There's always something to live for."

Sir Philip crossed his arms over his chest, and his expression chided her with laughter. "Are you trying to tell me that I should end this book with a wedding?"

"Better that than a funeral. Couldn't you make Genevieve somebody else's wife? A brother's, perhaps. Couldn't she be his brother's widow?"

"Absolutely not," he said, his tone falling from the bantering they'd been indulging in. "However," he said, lightening, "my hero has a best friend, a wise and kind minstrel. What if, with his dying breath, he commends them to each other. They'd marry, the lands would be secure—without a proper heir the king is sure to award them to the widow—and they'd be happy."

"Wouldn't the best friend know she didn't really love him?"

"She could leave him and enter a nunnery."

"No!" Camilla objected again. "She should be happy. Maybe she stopped loving your hero while he was away; I'll wager he never wrote a word while he was gone."

"I doubt it; he can't write."

"Well, then," she said, settling the matter. "It

sounds wonderful. I shall order a copy from the bookseller's as soon as it is printed."

"Much obliged, ma'am," he said with a bow. "You can read the first three chapters now, if you like. That is, if you can decipher my scrawl."

"May I?" she asked breathlessly. It seemed a very great honor. But when she took up the stack of paper and tried to read, she quickly saw that he'd not exaggerated the quality of his handwriting. "Perhaps in the morning," she said after a struggle. "When the light is better."

His laughter gave her hope that she'd not offended him. "Whenever and wherever you please, Miss Twainsbury."

"But I shall take this up with me," she said, picking up his book. "Though I shouldn't read it now; it will probably keep me awake until dawn."

"It's not so far off," he put in, glancing toward the gilt and silver clock, the balls of the regulator spinning around under a couple of cupids. "Did you come down only in search of a book?"

"Yes, I woke up suddenly." She didn't want to tell him that she'd been so hungry, though she did not think he'd take offense by assuming she wasn't satisfied with the meal she'd eaten under his roof.

"May I wish for you that you fall asleep as suddenly as you awoke. I would walk you to your door but . . ." He hesitated.

"Please don't trouble," Camilla said quickly. "I know the way." She paused, then asked the question that had been troubling her. "Sir Philip, why . . . I don't wish to seem ungrateful. You and Lady LaCorte have been more than kind to a stranger and yet . . . Pardon me, I don't quite know how to say what I am wondering."

"Perhaps you are wondering why my sister-in-law seems to have taken you in dislike, when you have done nothing whatever to harm her." His voice and face had lost all animation, becoming as cold as a bust sculpted from ice.

"I'm sure I'm imagining things," Camilla went on, reluctantly, sure it was nothing of the kind. "No doubt she is simply tired or out of sorts. Ladies in such condition are often prey to fancies, I believe."

"No, you are entirely correct and quite observant. My sister-in-law would prefer young ladies not come to this house. Not even friends of Tinarose are welcome here now."

"Why not?"

He rubbed his neck again, a habit that seemed to come upon him whenever he was at a loss for words. "I'm afraid it has to do with me."

"You?" she asked. For the first time, she realized what this meeting must look like to any observer. She, dressed in no more than wrapper and night-clothes, however thick and unrevealing, alone with a young and single gentleman who had long since removed coat and shoes. Many forced marriages had been made of less than this. Camilla moved back a little, holding his book against her breast.

"She's afraid you want to marry me," Sir Philip said.

CHAPTER EIGHT

"Marry you?" Camilla exclaimed. "We've only just met."

"Without wishing to seem conceited, there are some reasons for her concern."

Camilla wondered if this could mean he'd considered, even for a moment, the prospect of proposing to her. But that was impossible on such short acquaintance. "You are in the habit of asking strange young women to marry you?"

"No. I can truthfully state that I have never yet asked any woman to give up the joys of spinsterhood for the doubtful pleasure of being my wife. However, since my arrival in Bishop's Halt, there have been some . . . incidents."

"Incidents," she echoed. "What kind of incidents?"

"You must understand there are comparatively few single gentlemen in Bishop's Halt. Myself and Evelyn March are alone in our lack of wife. Naturally, this makes us objects of some interest to the young ladies of the town as well as their mothers." Though it was difficult to see by candlelight, Camilla could have sworn he was blushing like any maiden.

"You can't possibly mean that . . . Have they been throwing themselves at your head?"

"One feels so embarrassed for the poor things." She could tell he was definitely blushing now. "Twice I've been forced into the position of refusing offers for my hand if not my heart. One young lady, soon after my arrival in this house, attempted a ploy so underhanded that it was considered the best course for her mother to convey her out of the county afterward. You see, her mother was standing outside my door, concealed behind a large Chinese vase, whispering encouragement in no uncertain terms."

Camilla found herself choking quietly on a laugh.

"And what poor Evelyn has suffered from patients exaggerating their woes hardly bears thinking of. One young person actually pretended to have symptoms of the plague in order to force him into quarantine with her. Fortunately, he saw through the ruse in time."

Camilla could no longer strangle on a laugh; it burst through. Instantly, she pressed her fingers to her lips, stifling the sound, but could not forbear giggling. "How perfectly absurd," she said, little gasps and titters escaping despite her best efforts.

"It isn't actually funny," Sir Philip said, his own voice breaking with the strain of bottling up his laughter.

"No, no, of course not. How desperate those girls and their mothers must be. Mine would never permit me to act in such an ungenteel fashion."

"Desperate is the word for it. Since the war, there's such a surplus of eligible women, twelve for every ten men according to the *Times*. The competition for suitable husbands cannot help but be intensified."

"You just wish they wouldn't all focus on you."

"Exactly. I can have only one wife, according to the common usage of the country."

"Other nations arrange this sort of thing so much more sensibly," Camilla said, who had read in snatched private moments a book about the lands where polygamy was rife. Needless to say, she didn't approve a particle.

"I couldn't have a harem," he said. "I'm not so young as once I was."

"Poor Sir Philip. I had better leave you now and let you get your rest."

"Stay but one more moment," he said, touching her lightly on the elbow. "You mustn't think that my sister-in-law doesn't like you. She does not know you."

"I may prove to be a fortune hunter yet, Sir Philip."

"Not you," he said with such a warm, admiring look that Camilla found herself the one with reddened cheeks. "You never could have brought yourself all the way to my door in this snow if you cared only for yourself and for personal fortune. If I can draw upon your compassion for my sister-in-law and myself, I should consider myself highly fortunate."

"I am, of course, willing to do whatever lies in my poor power in order to make some recompense for your hospitality." Besides, she enjoyed talking to him openly like this. It was so unusually liberating to speak her mind without weighing every word on a scale of respectability.

"Then, do your best to befriend Beulah. She needs someone to listen to her and move her thoughts into a more cheerful frame. Between the burdens of her condition and the loss of my brother, she broods upon her woes. It was bad enough earlier in the year, but the death of poor Princess Charlotte has darkened her outlook further yet."

"I can see how that might happen." The tragic loss of the Heiress of England in childbed but three weeks before had been the leading topic at every gathering, and every detail of the funeral had been written over and discussed until they were as familiar as the details of one's own family life.

"If only Myron were here," Sir Philip said under his breath.

"But why?" she asked. "Surely as the wife of a naval officer, Lady LaCorte must be accustomed to . . . unless he was present for the births of his other children?"

"Only Tinarose. As is the case for most children of military men, they have scarcely seen him but for a few weeks at a time. This last visit was the longest he'd been home since he'd been beached waiting for his first real command—and that must be all of twenty years ago. Beulah was used to having command of the Manor and of her children."

"Yet still it must be hard for Lady LaCorte, knowing that this time he'll not come back."

"She thought him dead a hundred times before this. But it was the losing of all hope that seemed to depress her spirits the most. As if an invisible prop has been taken away. And then to have me inheriting on top of it all."

"You seem unobjectionable," Camilla said.

"Thank you." He bowed gravely. "But anyone would be objectionable under the circumstances. A husband lost at sea, a child on the way, three daughters to raise, and a none-too-well-loved brother-in-law now in the position of master in her husband's home. Who knows but that I might run mad and turn them all out into the snow."

"You never would," Camilla said, certain of it.

"Thank you for the vote of confidence," he answered with a grave nod of the head like any senior statesman. "My brother left a will quite ten years old, encouraging me to watch over my brother's family but in no way legally obligating me to do so. My sister-in-law lives with the constant anxiety of being so precariously settled. She knows she may always make her home here at the Manor, which she has decorated so lovingly, but knows also that if I marry, it may be to someone who will not honor his wishes. I hope I have more courage of character than to be swayed against Beulah, but more men have been fools than were ever wise."

"I shall certainly inform Lady LaCorte, should the matter arise, that I have no intention whatsoever of marrying you, Sir Philip." She couldn't help but wonder if all this was simply a clever man's way of warding off unwelcome female attentions.

"She won't believe you, but you may try. Of course, the whole issue may resolve itself, should the child she presently carries prove to be a boy. Then 'farewell, Sir Philip; welcome Mr. Philip LaCorte, author, traveler, and *bon vivant.*' "

"Yes, that's right. She might have a son."

"I pray for it every night," he said, the ring of sincerity in every word. "Confidentially, I was never cut out to bear a title. Perhaps one day, if I earn it myself by the writing of some fine book or other. But to bear it because Great-Grandpapa flattered the right king, no thank you. I leave that to Myron, curse him."

"Curse him?" Camilla echoed, shocked. Even

her mother, with all her cause for complaint about her late husband's gift for squandering whatever fortune came his way, never spoke ill of him after his death. Death was the Great Refurbisher. It removed all spots and stains, all slips and errors, turning the decedent into a shining glory that bore little resemblance to the fallible mortal of yesterday.

"Yes," he said, his voice hardening. "What business did he have taking up another command? He should have sold out and come home to stay."

"His duty—" She began, but he cut her off.

"Duty? He did that, and more, during the war like every decent man. But when war is over, a man must think of his family. If I had a wife, a wife I loved as dearly as my brother loved his, no power on earth but the defense of my country would take me away from her.

"Most men would feel that way," Camilla said, moved by the depth of sensibility he showed. "At least, I hope they would."

"Myron didn't. It wasn't duty that made him go back. It was the sea, the love of the sea. Even when he was a boy, that's the only thing he ever thought about. We're a hundred and fifty miles from the nearest ocean, yet it beat in his blood and filled his brain until he was crazy with it." He chuckled ruefully. "Do you know—he ran away when he was nine. There'd been some discussion of his future career, I think. Father wanted him to be political. Myron made it all the way to Dover before Father caught him."

"What happened?" Camilla asked, seeing the young boy with determination in his eyes crossing the countless miles between himself and his destination. How many rides did he cajole out of passing farmers? How many nights must he have slept "rough," and how many countless miles would he have walked? She couldn't think of anything that she wanted so much that she'd suffer such hardship. Nothing, that was, except the one thing she'd wished for above all others. Perhaps that had been young Myron's goad. A love he could express in no other way except through suffering to achieve it.

"He'd already persuaded some poor old captain to take him on as cabin boy. The only way Father could bring him home was to swear on a Bible that Myron could go to sea when he was older."

"You must have admired him," Camilla said softly, hearing the love behind every word.

"He was my older brother. He went where no one else dared go, and I followed. He never understood the things that drove me, any more than I ever understood his obsessions. To me, the sea is just something to travel over as swiftly and as safely as human ingenuity can allow."

"I don't blame you for that. My sister hates it, too."

"You know what it is to have family, Miss Twainsbury. When you come to it, who is closer than a brother? I've shared many an adventure with other men, some of whom I grew to know so well that we could move in complete silence, judging our actions by no more than a pointed finger or a quickened breath. But Myron and I shared common blood, and that's something that does not alter, even when all other bonds are shattered."

He fell silent, looking into the black corners of the room as if he were looking for someone. Camilla felt as if she hardly dared to breathe, fearing to disrupt the communication between the living man and the one gone far out of reach. At last his gaze came back to her.

"I have a sister, sir," she said. "Women are more

fortunate than men in this. We share so much that is common to us all. I sometimes think a woman could fly to the moon, and so long as there were females there, we would understand each other perfectly well. No doubt they gossip the same on the moon as on earth and share stories that no man may ever hear."

His expression lightened. "You make women sound as if they all belong to some secret order, that of Eleusinian Mysteries perhaps."

"I don't know what that is."

"Oh, secret Greek rites in honor of some virgin goddess. No man was supposed to look upon them."

"Well, we must keep something for ourselves alone," Camilla said with a laugh that perhaps held more mystery in it than she'd intended. She hoped he wouldn't think she was attempting to flirt with him. It was past time to call this interesting *tête-à-tête* to an end.

She yawned.

"You're tired and no wonder. Leaving you standing here in a draught while I rattle on. You should have reproved me sooner."

"Oh, no," she said with genuine warmth. "It's been most interesting. You've answered my questions, and I'm grateful."

"It's I should be grateful to you." He changed the subject, feeling, perhaps, their intimacy had grown too quickly. "Tell me," he said, like any genial host, "have you everything you want in your room?"

"Yes. Mavis and your niece have made my room as cozy as my own at home. I don't mind saying that at first I was a trifle hesitant to get into bed this evening. I thought for a certainty that I would find a hairbrush in my bed or that it had been made up apple-pie fashion."

"Why? Has anyone . . . if my nieces have been less than welcoming . . ."

She only smiled, wishing she'd not brought the subject up.

"Not my nieces, then. The servants? Have they been impertinent?"

"Oh, no, not at all. Now that you've explained things," Camilla said quickly.

"So, they were less than kind. I don't count Mavis; she'd serve tea to the devil himself if he looked as though he could stand a cup."

"They weren't unkind," Camilla said hurriedly. "On the contrary, Mrs. Lamsard, for one, could not have been kinder. Of course they would choose to protect their mistress. Anyone would have done the same."

"I shall have a word with them come the morning."

Camilla laid her hand delicately on his folded arm. "Pray don't. If I were going to remain here, perhaps I should use you for my champion. But as Nanny Mallow and I will return to her cottage as soon as the weather clears . . ."

"Nonsense," he said from deep in his chest. "You and she will stay here, as our guest. Nanny will have every comfort, far better than that old cottage with the wind prying loose the shingles."

"I'm sure she would not wish to impose upon you."

"There's no imposition in the case. It's settled."

Seeing that nothing she could say at this juncture could alter his mind-set, Camilla thanked him and said good night. Before she could depart, however, he caught her by the hand. Giving it a firm, respectful shake, he stopped and stood looking down at her fingers, lying unresistingly in his. "We must surely be destined for friendship," he said. "In the course of an evening, we have discussed history, literature, love, and war and found, if not uniformity of opinion, at least respectful challenge. Thank you, Miss Twainsbury. I cannot remember when I was last so happy to meet someone."

"Thank you, Sir Philip," she said. He released her, and she started for the door. On the threshold, she turned back a moment, wishing to speak. But the words she wanted to say must surely seem too bold from a maiden to a gentleman. Her mother would certainly think so. Until Camilla could be quite sure that her own ideas of the world could stand against her mother's, she thought she'd better allow her mother's teachings to win the day.

"Good night, then, Sir Philip."

Despite her interrupted night, Camilla woke early. Stretching out in bed, she found that she'd awakened with a particularly contented smile on her face. At first, she thought it was because no one had roused her from bed at daybreak to sweep a grate or start a fire. She had no posset to brew, no breakfast to make, no list of duties to perform. True, when she removed to Nanny Mallow's house, she would cheerfully do all she could, more than she was asked, to help the older woman, especially with her injuries. In a great house like this, however, any attempt to assist would be met with very proper refusal and might alienate the very people she wanted to assist.

Camilla hoped she was not so shallow as to revel in the mere physical luxuries of the Manor. Servants and fine furnishings were all very well, but if they were going to corrupt her essential nature, she'd be better off without them. Examining her soul closely, Camilla decided that she was in no danger from an eiderdown coverlet and a fine carpet. Her happiness this morning must spring from a different source.

Pressing her pillows into a bolster shape behind her neck, Camilla recalled her interrupted night. Sir Philip's slow revelation of his different facets made him much more interesting than the surface word "charming" that she'd first applied to him. Last night, there'd been true emotion in his voice several times as he expressed his thoughts. He had treated her throughout their acquaintance as a friend; even more so, as an equal.

"Heady stuff," she told herself, making it a warning. She'd never had a man treat her as if he valued her for the reason, common sense, and gift of observation that were her dearest possessions. These three counselors joined now to tell her that though her observations of Sir Philip promised that he was as honest and forthright as he appeared, her reason reminded her that no person could ever be less than complex, while her common sense warned against any impulsive emotional tie. Even friendship came with dangers. Far wiser to hold back from furthering this friendship until she knew whether they'd ever meet again.

Camilla promised herself that she would be wise and cautious. Yet even if they never met again from this day until the passing away of the world, she would feel that she'd made a friend.

Someone had laid out on the end of the bed one of Camilla's own dresses, the wrinkles caused by packing having been pressed smooth. Looking around, she saw her own hairbrush and comb on the dressing table, her own bottle of apple-water beside them, even the book she'd packed by mistake. Camilla reproached herself for having slept so soundly that a maid had been able to do all this, like a fairy at morning light, without disturbing her in the slightest. In something of a fuss, she began to dress.

Once attired in her lilac sarsenet, the fashionable white trimming at the neckline and sleeves never betraying that it had been sewn on at home, she made sure her hair was neatly dressed in its usual smooth knot. There was no point in attempting anything that would betray her desire to be as elegant as her surroundings.

As she had been dressing, she noticed strange noises in the hall outside her door. They had passed away after a little while, sometime between her drawing on her stockings and sitting down before the mirror, and she'd thought no more about them. Now they returned, rustlings, whisperings, running footsteps. She wondered if these were the fairies who had worked so many wonders while she slept. In this curious house, she wouldn't be surprised to find some young maids lurking in the hallways when they should be working. Yet, it didn't sound exactly like that.

Tiptoeing herself, Camilla approached the door. Placing her ear against the white panels, she listened intently. When she judged the sounds to be nearest, she suddenly twisted the knob. Opening the door, she surprised two very young maidens, indeed.

"Oh!" said the oldest, grasping her sister by the hand. "You shouldn't do that; it might make her scream."

"Who?" Camilla asked, smiling at them. Dressed alike in tight red pelisses covering them from neck to waist, the two youngest daughters of the Manor gazed up at her from very similar dark blue eyes. They looked like a pair of kittens, unsure whether to hiss or to purr.

"Her," the girl said with a nod toward her smaller sister. "She has the loudest scream in the world. It shakes the windows. Uncle said that if she screams today, it might cause a *navalanche.*"

"An avalanche?"

"Yes. Do you know what that is?"

"I think so. Do you?"

Two similar dark heads were shaken.

"Oh," said Camilla, who had been offering the little girl a chance to show off her superior knowledge. "Well, I believe it's a large fall of snow, very dangerous."

"Oh, then, we had one last night."

"I didn't mean that kind of snowfall. More like, all at once . . . down a mountainside? Quite destructive."

"Hmm," said the elder, whose name Camilla could not recall. She remembered Tinarose saying something about how her sister's names were simpler than her own. She felt sure the littlest one's name was Grace. She'd thought at the time that it sounded too adult for so small a person.

Now she grabbed Camilla's hand and pulled. "Come and see," she said. Her small hand was slightly sticky and surprisingly strong. Towed along, the other sister coming behind, Camilla didn't want to seem petulant by demanding to know where they were taking her. *Perhaps,* she thought hopefully, as they went downstairs, *they are taking me to breakfast.*

"Look!" said Grace as they reached the ground floor.

"At what?" Camilla asked, after looking about her obediently.

"At the window," the older one said impatiently.

Camilla looked and, at first glance, saw nothing but the faint grayish light of a snowy morning. It must be earlier than she'd thought. The clock in her room could not have been set properly, though it had been wound so that its cheerful ticking could be heard. It had said eight-forty-five when she'd awakened, but it must be closer to dawn.

Then she looked again and yet once more. No gray light of early morning this—it was snow, piled as high as the second row of mullions that divided the windows into neat squares. Whatever sunlight there was came in filtered through the pressing weight of the snow.

"We're going to sled later," the older sister said. "Mr. Samson has promised us two big trays."

"How thrilling," Camilla commented, unable to take her eyes from the window.

"I see they've shown you," Sir Philip said from behind her. "Merridew says it's the most snow he's seen since he was a boy, though I think the winter of 1814 was colder."

"I remember that very well," Camilla said. "We had to sacrifice an old card table when the wood gave out."

"Fortunately, we won't have to go to that extreme," he said, solemnly giving a hand to each of his clamoring nieces. "Though, frankly, I can think of several pieces that could be spared," he added, his undertone further masked by the little girls' demands that he venture into the snow with them.

"Not until the stable lads and the gardeners have dug out all the doorways," he said. "And Cook is making gingerbread dollies and seems to be at rather a loss on how to decorate them properly. She seems to want to use sultanas for their vest buttons."

This, it seemed, was some kind of offense. The two children ran off, protesting. Sir Philip turned back to Camilla, who, suddenly, felt shy. "It is a good thing that Dr. March left last night," she said,

choosing a neutral subject. "It would be too bad if
someone needed him and he could not get out."

"He's more likely to be needed here. My sister-
in-law is quite near her time." He looked at her curiously. "You're smiling. Why?"

"Oh, merely . . ." She remembered with what
openness they'd spoken last night and could not
bring herself to retreat entirely into the common
usage of a pair of strangers. "It's only that my
mother sent me away so I should not be present at
the birth of my niece. And here I am. . . ."

"Awaiting another birth? Fate must have made it
so, Miss Twainsbury."

"I'm not sure I believe in fate, Sir Philip."

"Ah, but does it believe in you?"

CHAPTER NINE

Camilla felt that her first duty, even before breakfast, was to visit Nanny Mallow. Assured by Mavis that the patient was awake and eager for visitors, Camilla knocked, wishing she had some flowers or calf's foot jelly to bring to a sufferer. Her mother made wonderfully clear jellies.

"You're looking very well," Camilla said, smiling on the wrinkled face turned up to hers. Nanny seemed to expect more, so Camilla bent down and kissed her surprisingly soft cheek. She felt a little off balance about it; she'd not been raised to expect or to give easy kisses.

"It's like a miracle to be so safe and comfortable after so hard a time."

"Well, you look blooming," Camilla said stoutly. "If I thought it would improve my looks at all, I'd do the same as you. Only with my fortune, I should be more likely to sprain my nose rather than a knee."

"Oh, I know just the right treatment for a sprained nose," Nanny Mallow said with her young-old laughter. Camilla didn't know whether to take her seriously or not.

"I hope you are feeling much better this morning," Camilla said.

Nanny grasped Camilla's sleeve, and leaning forward, she turned a sly glance toward the nurse. "She pretends to be so stern and unfeeling, but she's as gentle as a mother."

Mrs. Duke growled a little, like a dog making sure no one makes off with her special bone. Then she whisked away to stand by the fireplace, poking at some aromatic mixture in a pot set down among the ashes.

Nanny Mallow laughed and settled back again against her mounded pillows and cushions. A twinge of pain crossed her face. "I never would have believed so many bits of ourselves are strung through the knee," she said. "Even if I don't use it or go anywhere near it, it starts aching all over again. Mind you, I'm glad to be clean and warm—two I thought I'd never see anymore—but I wish this clever doctor'd explain how come when I wiggle m'left thumb, m'right knee starts giving me three kinds of gyp."

"I know it must be hard to find the patience to wait for yourself to heal."

"I know, I know," she said irritably. "That's the same advice I give m'self. Can't say I pay much attention."

"None at all," Mrs. Duke muttered under her breath but clear enough to be heard.

"Never mind her. How are you getting on, Miss Camilla?"

"Everyone is treating me like an old friend already."

"Hmmm, could be good that, or could be bad. Which is it?"

"Oh, good, very good. I feel quite one of the family already. Sir Philip—" She began and then hesitated. These fearsome old women could build a whole tragic fairy tale out of two chance-fallen words. "Sir Philip has been more than gracious," she said quickly.

The two women exchanged glances. Mrs. Duke twitched her shoulder and turned again to the mixture on the hearth. "He's a very pleasant gentleman," Nanny Mallow allowed. "Very good to his dependents. Sent me down a venison pasty last time he shot a deer in the park."

"I'm sure he takes his position very seriously," Camilla agreed, thinking that last night he'd seemed almost reluctant to take on his brother's fallen burden.

Nanny Mallow tried to adjust her position on the pillows, sucking in her breath through her teeth at the twinge of pain that accompanied her every movement.

"Let me help you, Nanny," Camilla said, straightening a fallen cushion.

"It passes me," Nanny said. "Would you say I so much as moved that knee?"

"If you would lay still, nothing would hurt," Mrs. Duke said.

"If I'm going to lie that still," Nanny Mallow retorted, "I might as well have died."

Camilla tried to turn the conversation into more cheerful channels. "Have you heard about the snow?"

"*She* claims 'tis higher than m'head," Nanny said, scornful of such exaggerated claims.

"That's more or less true. Sir Philip says you and I will be his guests while it lasts. The stable lads are trying to clear paths, but he says the drive is too long to be attempted just yet."

Nanny Mallow nodded portentously. "There. That's what I mean about him. Kind, generous to a fault, and quite good-looking if you like that kind. I always preferred 'em dark and brooding with a smile that could turn a girl's heart inside out. That's not the sort to marry, though." She sighed at the thought with reminiscent pleasure. "You could do worse, Miss Camilla."

"I?"

The older woman took hold of her hand. "Now, don't be shy 'bout this sort of thing. If a girl can't talk to her elders about love, she's left on her own, and that's a bad place to be when you're young 'n' foolish."

"No fool like an old fool," Mrs. Duke said from her corner. She'd brought out a skein of gray wool and was knitting along at great speed.

"Hush, Portia Duke. You could go farther and fare worse for a mistress than any girl raised by my Miss Lolly."

Camilla balked at the thought of anyone calling her mother "Lolly." As a matter of fact, she couldn't think of anyone anymore who called her mother anything save "Mrs. Twainsbury." Thus she lost her moment to declare that nothing would make her think of marrying Sir Philip.

"My Miss Lolly was a bit wild when she was a girl, maybe so, but she soon learned the error of her ways. Life's been more than a little hard on her, but she soon learned that being down-to-earth and no-nonsense was the way to get on."

"Wild?" Camilla coughed. "My mother?"

"Oh, not a hurly-burly girl by any means, just a bit . . . neither to lead nor to drive. The more she was told she couldn't nor shouldn't, the more headstrong she grew. I knew how to handle her, but those parents of hers . . ." She clicked her tongue in derision. "She never would have run off with your father if they'd let him come calling at the house like a Christian 'stead of forcing 'em into meeting behind hedges and in the church on Monday mornings."

Camilla pressed her fingers hard to her temple, feeling as if the top of her head was about to spin off. She'd never heard a word of this before. Her parents—a runaway marriage?

"I hadn't realized," she began carefully, "that my Feldon grandparents were opposed to my father."

"Oh, they came around by the time Linnet was born, but for the first year or two, not a word passed between 'em. My Miss Lolly didn't care a twig. She wasn't the sort to come crawling back on her hands 'n' knees, no, not if she were starving, which they pretty near did that first year. They lived in lodgings not far from where I was employed at the time, so I'd see 'em now and again with the hind end of a loaf or a few scones in my basket. Not a shred had she but the clothes she'd gone away in, and a few things she'd bundled into a bandbox, but she was just as gay and merry as any bride should be."

Gay? Merry? It was hard to imagine her stern, proper mother as a spoiled, ardent girl determined to throw her heart over the windmill. Perhaps Nanny was confusing her mother with some other young girl she'd attended. "This was in Portsmouth, Nanny?"

"No. No, Canterbury. My employer lived in the shadow of the cathedral, or so his wife liked to say. Proud, stuck-up piece she was, no better than she ought to be, as I learned later."

Camilla breathed a sigh of relief. "My sister was born in Portsmouth, not Canterbury. You must be thinking of someone else, Nanny, not my mother."

"Not your mother? Pshaw! Little Lolly was my first charge as a sole nursery maid. I'd worked under Nanny Langton as undernursery maid at Viscount D'Arby's town house—coo, she was a tartar if ever there was one. Regular Attila the Hun in petticoats." She shook her head. "Finicky, my heavens! Always turned out neat as a cat in pattens, and that's not such a simple matter when you're in charge of five holy terrors all under the age of six. I stayed out my year, but that was quite enough."

"So you went to my grandparents?"

"That's it. Came to them just after the month. Tiny thing she was. First baby I ever saw with curls, sausage curls, and she hardly born. I remember 'em curling up again, spry as springs, after the parson wet her little head. She never cried a tear either, just smiled up and tried to catch the parson's linen. I remember brushing those curls round 'n' round m'finger. She kept them all her life, too. Why, I couldn't forget my first baby."

"No, of course not," Camilla said soothingly, more confident yet that Nanny had grown confused. Though she'd but rarely seen her mother without the stern widow's caps she affected, she knew that there was not now, nor could there ever have been, curls in her hair. She wore it in smooth bands without even a fringe to soften it. Camilla well recalled how gravely her mother had read her a lecture on vanity when she had, several years ago, wantonly cut her hair so that it curled softly on her cheeks as she'd seen in a ladies' magazine. It had been rather flattering, or so Camilla had thought, but when her hair grew out, she did not cut it again.

Once more seeking to change the subject, Camilla brought up something that she knew would interest Nanny Mallow. "I wanted to tell you that Rex is doing very well."

"You saw him today?"

"No, last night. He was lying by the fire, looking happy as the king he was named for. Chasing rabbits in his sleep, if I'm any judge."

"In the house? Oh, ho, her la'ship won't care for that!"

"He was there by Sir Philip's invitation."

"That's all right, then," Nanny said, ignoring the snort from the corner. "You see how kind he is. And so good with the children, though well I know what a nuisance little girls can be to the gentlemen. But he always takes time to speak to them, and I know he had one of little Grace's daubs framed and hung up in his dressing room. She said it was him on his favorite horse, but bless her little heart, it looked no more like that than a plate of cold vermicelli."

"Aye, he's fond enough of them," Mrs. Duke said. She sat knitting like a chorus out of some Greek play. "Considerin' how he never came nigh 'em 'til the master died. Off gallivanting t' the four corners of the world, he was, and her la'ship here on her own with three little 'uns to raise up in the way they should go. Not so much as a penny whistle at Christmastide either."

"Gallivanting? Gallivanting? When you've heard with your own ears Dr. Marsh say how he saw him wounded in that sink o' sin, Paris, France." The amount of venom infused into the name of the French capital could have poisoned the whole city.

"And whose ears would I use, Mrs. Mallow? I heard him, right enough, but who's to say how he came by that wound? He weren't in no regiment *I* ever heard of," she said with the air of one who studied the Army List regularly for her light entertainment.

Though it undoubtedly fell under the heading of the strictly banned "gossiping with the servants," Camilla added her might to the conversation. "Oh, Dr. March told that story at dinner last night."

She suddenly felt like an innocent fishing boat facing the open gunports of an enemy, so attentive did the two ladies become.

"Did he, now? You never told me that, Portia Duke," Nanny Mallow accused.

"I didn't know. If my Eunice has been keeping secrets from her ma . . ."

"Oh, only Mr. Samson was in the room at the time," Camilla said, not wishing to cause the maid difficulties.

"He won't gossip," Nanny Mallow said. "That's the worst of him. So what did Dr. March say?"

Camilla told them the tale simply, without any of the flourishes the doctor had added. The two women nodded at each other like wise Mandarins. " 'Them what lives by the sword dies by the sword,' " Mrs. Duke proclaimed. "That's in the Bible an' true as the day it was handed down."

"Well, he didn't die by any sword," Nanny shot back with incontrovertible logic. " 'Twas most likely a knife, and he didn't die anyway. Probably was robbed by one of them nasty, murdering French. Use a knife as soon as look at you if not sooner. Poor lamb's lucky not to be buried in a pauper's grave with a foreign priest a-mumbling over him an' all his bits and bobs handed over to the French king."

"What would he want with Sir Philip's old clothes?" Mrs. Duke scoffed. "Besides, it's more'n likely he had a fallin' out with some of those artist fellows. Geniuses, ha! Low's what I call 'em. D'you remember the time he brought those friends of his here? Poor as church mice, the lot of 'em, and not a vail did they hand out while they were here."

"Oh, come. You told me that was more 'n fifteen years ago. Boys at school never have any pocket money that doesn't go for sweeties and other such truck."

"I don't care; I can't stand meanness in the gentry."

"Never mind her," Nanny Mallow said with a wise nod toward Camilla. "I know a good man when I sees one. Look for the kind eyes, that's what I say. If a man has kind eyes, then he's good all the way through. You can't falsify that. I've known a few who acted like they had the milk o' human kindness flowing through 'em like the Thames but had mean piggy eyes. Every time, that meanness came out in one way or another. Maybe it's turning out your only child; maybe it's not giving more 'n bread and skilly when you promised to help the starving."

"You're right there, Mrs. Mallow," Mrs. Duke said. "Why, I even knew a woman once who would rap a guinea against the poorbox, making everyone think she'd dropped it in, when she never gave more than a shilling if so much. The way everyone used to praise her for being so large hearted would shame the devil. Cheat the poor now, I told her when I left her service, but you'll wish you'd given all them guineas twice over when you're gone to your reward."

"And did she have mean little eyes?" Nanny asked, eager to hear her sometimes rival agree with her.

"Not so you'd notice. Everyone said she was a pretty little thing. But I knew better. Handsome is as handsome does."

"I'm hardly concerned that Sir Philip will prove to be mean," Camilla said when it seemed the argument would continue. "Not when he has already been so very kind and more than kind to you and me."

"I'm glad you recognized his good qualities. Dwell on them and maybe you'll see what a fine husband he'd make for you." Mrs. Duke began to cough halfway through this speech. Nanny Mallow didn't let it stop her.

"You're just the right age to be thinking of marriage, not so young that you're a fool, and not so old that you'll be turned into one. Don't let foolish fancies of some knight on a white horse blind you to your true interest. Sir Philip is a fine man and . . . Portia Duke, are you dying? Then do it quietlike," she added, turning her head to seek out her friend.

There she paused, such an odd look of arrest on her face, that Camilla could not choose but turn also. Even before she did so, however, she had a sudden premonition as to who she would see.

Lady LaCorte still had her hand on the doorknob, so Camilla knew a flicker of hope that she'd not heard Nanny Mallow's advice. The elderly woman had been speaking softly and rapidly, so that even Camilla, who sat so close, had occasionally lost a word. Even her ladyship's expression, being cold and impassive, gave no hint of whether she'd heard Nanny Mallow setting out Sir Philip's qualifications for Camilla's husband.

Yet, some other sense told Camilla that Lady LaCorte had heard every word. Some barely screened expression of distaste had passed over that aristocratic, if slightly swollen, face when she glanced at Camilla.

"I stopped by to see if you have all you require, Mrs. Mallow."

" 'Tis very good of your la'ship. I'm tolerable comfortable now."

"You relieve my mind. And yourself, Miss Twainsbury? I trust you had a peaceful night."

Did she know about her midnight meeting with Sir Philip? Camilla tried to squelch a guilty conscience, reminding herself that the meeting was by chance and not by the calculation Lady LaCorte seemed intent on suspecting. "Exceedingly peaceful, Lady LaCorte."

"I believe you have not yet taken the time to eat breakfast. If you would care to go down for it now, I could accompany you."

Camilla recalled, with a truly guilty start, that her mother had often told her that in country houses, breakfast is served in the breakfast room between the hours of eight o'clock and ten-thirty. Camilla, very young, had commented that it never took her two and a half hours to eat her breakfast. Her mother had then explained that these extended hours were for the benefit of both late-rising and early-rising guests, so that neither might be inconvenienced by the other's queer hours.

It must be nearly ten-thirty now, and Lady LaCorte had come in search of her so that she might eat without discommoding the servants who must be waiting to clear up in order to prepare for the noon collation.

She kissed Nanny Mallow because the woman seemed to expect it, gave her duty to Mrs. Duke, and followed the silent mistress of the household down the steps. She was framing in her mind various ways of assuring her ladyship that she would never consider marrying Sir Philip when the arrival of the gentleman himself forestalled her.

"Would you believe it, Beulah? Though I awoke hungry as a hunter, I completely forgot to take any breakfast until just now. I hope there are some sausages left. Mrs. Lamsard," he said to Camilla, "makes the sort of sausages they must eat in heaven."

"What have you been doing, Philip?" his sister-in-law asked gravely.

"Trying to keep those damn-fool stable lads from burying themselves and me under six feet of snow. I had to tell them I'd discharge the next one who threw a snowball while on duty."

"Did that dissuade them?" Camilla asked.

He grinned. "Considering I just shook half a ton of snow from my collar, on the whole, I'd say not."

"Then, you should discharge them," his sister-in-law said.

"Where are they to go in weather like this? If I discharge them, I still have to feed them, and they don't have to work. If I keep them on, at least they earn their bread." He uncovered a silver toast rack and offered it to Camilla. "Will you come sledding with the children and me? Tinarose thinks she's too old for such children's games, but if you go, I'll wager she will."

With a sudden nostalgic mellowing, Lady LaCorte looked interested. "Are the girls sledding on those big silver trays?"

"Samson said he'd lend them. Do you mind?"

Lady LaCorte gave her half laugh and shook her head. "I remember doing that, oh, quite twenty years ago. My mother was horrified to see us all, hoydens and shy buds alike, go screaming down the hill on her best silver trays. I don't recall whether she was more afraid for us or for the plate."

She turned toward Camilla. "Do go, Miss Twainsbury. It's an experience you will long delight in."

"Thank you. I can't remember ever trying it. But then, we have no trays large enough to hold me. My mother does not entertain very much and never on a grand scale."

"Nor do we, anymore," Lady LaCorte said with a return to her melancholy. "I'm confident, however, that no harm will come to the trays, or to the girls."

"Their poor uncle, however . . ." Sir Philip began. Catching Camilla's eye, he groaned a little, artistically. "The girls may ride down, but old Uncle Philip is the one who hauls them back up the hill. Not just once, mind, but dozens of times, almost every one of which is the precursor to 'just one more.' "

Camilla instinctively shielded her eyes with her hand as she stepped out into the Manor's kitchen yard. The stable boys had slaved away to clear a path from the stables, so that they could get something to eat, while the house servants, two footmen that Camilla hadn't seen before, had worked down from the house. As usual with such endeavors, the two paths had missed each other by a good margin so that the paths snaked around the yard before joining up. To the two younger girls, it was like a snow maze made just for them.

Cheeks wildly abloom with roses, little noses wiped frequently on balled-up handkerchiefs, Grace and Nelly romped around the yard, apparently enjoying running across unblemished crust in order to admire their tracks. The sight of their uncle brought them running.

"Are you ready yet?" Grace asked, fairly dancing with impatience.

"What do you suppose?" he asked in return, pointing to a slat-sided box stacked with five silver trays.

A chorus of cheering broke out, seemingly from more than two little throats, as echoes broke back from the bricks that enclosed half the yard. "Let's go," Nelly commanded, tugging at his hand.

"Now, wait a moment," he said, crouching down to their level, the skirts of his greatcoat spreading around him. "We have to make a few things plain first. Are you listening, Nelly? Grace?" They nodded gravely. "What about you, Miss Twainsbury?" he asked, looking up at her.

"Oh, certainly, Sir Philip." She arranged her expression to be most closely attentive.

"You're to stay with me; no running off to look at things, even if you see the world's most admirable rabbit. Understood?" He gave an extra stern look at little Grace. This seemed to have some relevance to her, for she hung her head and looked guilty. "The snow is very deep in some places, so please walk only where I tell you. The fastest are to walk with the slowest, and we leave as soon as one of us is tired. No whinging or begging to stay."

"I never whinge," Camilla said proudly in answer to his questioning glance. "And I shouldn't dream of begging."

"Furthermore," he added, "I'm the captain of this little expedition so no mutiny. Orders are orders. Understood?"

Two small heads nodded in their heavy winter caps, noses glowing brightly as coals. "Aye, aye, sir," Camilla said with an imitation salute.

"Remind me to show you how to do that properly," he said.

Camilla laughed. "Am I under orders already?"

"You are. Forward, march!"

With Sir Philip in the lead, a stout stick in his hand to feel for soft spots, followed by Camilla helping the little girls over the difficult terrain, and the stoutest of the two footmen trudging behind with the box of five trays, they were a strange little procession heading out for adventure.

Camilla spared a smile for her own appearance in the parade. She'd surely qualify as the clown. This time, instead of Mavis Duke's oversized boots, she wore a pair of her hostess's riding boots which, rising to her calf, kept the snow out but which would never be restored to the proper gloss after this treatment. Lady LaCorte had claimed not to care, saying her feet had grown too large with this last pregnancy to ever allow her to wear the boots again. Over her quilted spenser, Camilla wore an old multicaped coat which Sir Philip had hailed on first glimpse as having formerly belonged to himself.

"I was the proudest buck in three counties when the tailor delivered that monstrosity to my door. I fancied myself a Nonpareil, a veritable down-the-road man. Oh, well, everyone is entitled to some youthful folly, and that poor coat was one of my finest hours."

"It's certainly warm," Camilla said, holding up her arms. The sleeves draped over her knuckles so that she looked as if she had arms a mile long.

"It looks more becoming on you, Miss Twainsbury, than it ever did on me," he said gallantly. Raising his hands, he twitched the collar, so upstanding that the points all but groomed her eyebrows, so that it lay flat between her shoulder blades like a falling lace collar in one of the portraits of Charles the First. "Better. You might start a fashion."

"Not for bonnets, I'm afraid," Camilla said with another laugh. Her hostess had kindly lent her the loudest Scotch bonnet Camilla had ever seen. Of screaming orange and lime green, it bore a cockade of scarlet ribbon but had the merit of being exceedingly warm. Camilla felt sure Lady LaCorte had never worn the thing.

"It looks a bit familiar. I seem to recall a fancy dress party which my brother attended as Goliath whom, for some reason, he envisioned as a Scotsman."

"Captain LaCorte was a tall gentleman?"

"Shorter than myself by some inches, yet it was I who went as David and he as Goliath. He had the whole party roaring with laughter. Of course, we were only lads then."

Outside the yard, the clean white snow wore a sparkle of diamond dust everywhere except deep in the blue shadows. Any breeze sent a fine powder swirling up into the fresh, nose-prickling air. They had gone only a very little distance, Camilla's hem sweeping brush marks in the snow, when a shout of "Wait for me" made them all turn.

Still tying the flyaway strings of her bonnet under her chin, Tinarose came running toward them. "Please, Uncle Philip. May I come, too?"

"Of course," he said, pleased. Camilla noticed that he did not tease his niece by referring to her earlier pronouncement that sledding was for the children.

When they reached the sledding hill at last, Camilla taxed Sir Philip with his real reason for bringing the footman. After all three girls had gone sailing down the hill, their hands gripping

the chased silver handles tightly, screams of terror-
ized delight shredding the wooded calm, she noticed that it was not the uncle who stood waiting at
the bottom of the hill.

"Well," he said without a trace of remorse, "who
has better calf muscles, a man whose career it is to
walk up and down stairs and be willing for any labor,
or a poor writerly fellow who scribbles all day in an
easy chair?"

"Considering that you haven't even the decency
to be out of breath after a mile-long tramp through
deep snow . . ."

"Come, come. You exaggerate. Besides which—" He
broke off and began gasping like an extremely old
man attempting to climb a mountain. "My reaction is merely somewhat delayed due to . . . due to
not being wishful to distress the children."

"You are all consideration," Camilla said, gliding one, two steps behind him, just out of his eye-
sight. By the time he turned to address another
remark to her, she'd stooped and gathered together
an enormous snowball. She stood there, weighing
it in her hand, calculating whether she should
throw it or not.

"Miss Twainsbury . . . Camilla . . . pray . . ."

"Does a man with such an excellent line of hum-
bug as your uncle deserve a faceful of snow?" she
asked as the two youngest girls reappeared over
the crest of the hill, their silver sleds tied together
and the ropes over the footman's shoulder. Tinarose
appeared an instant later, having brought up her
own sled.

Instantly appraising the situation, they with one
voice shouted, "yes!" and, gathering more ammu-
nition, fired a fast and furious volley at a defense-
less Sir Philip. His hat flew down the slope. He
growled, paddling clear his face, then made alarm-

ing feints and attempts to grab each of his little nieces. Grace and Nelly screamed, laughed, and, seizing their sleds again from the footman, made off down the hill. Grace tumbled out of her sled at the bottom. Her surprised cry reached them faintly.

"I'll go," Tinarose said. Forgetting her dignity, she threw herself stomach-down on the largest sled and raced down the hill to her sister's succor.

"Yes, sir," the footman said in answer to his master's nod. But judging by the whoop he let go as he schussed away, he did not begrudge his orders too greatly.

Sir Philip turned slowly toward Camilla after seeing Tinarose wave to show that Grace, now up and apparently eager for another go, was perfectly well. "As the ringleader of this act of mutiny," he said with a quarter-deck rasp in his throat, as he shook off the snow from his shoulders, "what sentence d'you deserve, Able Seaman Twainsbury?"

"Able Seaman? I should be at least an officer."

"B'God, you should. Very well. For bravery in the field, as of last night, I hearby promote you to Lieutenant."

"Thank you," she said with a curtsey.

"Very well, Lieutenant. What sentence shall I pronounce for the high crime of throwing snowballs at your superior officer?"

"I don't know; let me think." She glanced around at sky, snow-burdened trees, and the stamp marks of feet and sleds all around. At the bottom of the hill, the riders were sorting themselves out.

With a laughing smile, she turned her gaze again to him and surprised an intense, studying expression in his eyes as he looked at her. He seemed to be asking her a question without words. He stood somehow much closer than she'd thought.

Camilla felt slightly out of breath, as if she'd run a long way and come to a sudden stop. They had been bantering so lightly, enjoying each other's company, and then, like the first sea breeze that gives notice of the tide's turning, this change.

Poised on the edge of the snowy hill, Camilla knew that if Philip reached out his hand to her, she'd be forced to make a choice she had no wish to make so soon. He looked as if he might speak, but she didn't permit him to go beyond the first syllable of her name.

"What better answer to mutiny in the ranks than escape?" she said, turning away. Seizing the fifth tray, standing abandoned on the edge of the hill, Camilla sat down quickly and pushed off as she'd seen the others do. Instantly, she was flying along much faster than she'd anticipated and had not time to do more than notice Sir Philip's last-second attempt to keep her from going over.

At the last instant, the tray spun her around backward as she shot over a snow-buried hump. The others scattered as she blew past them. Another bump came up fast. She and the tray parted company.

Spitting snow, Camilla sat up, shaking out her arms. A throbbing spot on her hip told her there would be bruises come the morning. As the others raced to her, she looked up and laughed to see Sir Philip, half out of control, come careering down the hillside.

"Are you all right?" he demanded, moving the children aside gently and reaching down to haul her to her feet.

She came up by the strength of his right arm. "I think I need more practice."

"We'll see that you get it."

CHAPTER TEN

Camilla wrote to her mother that afternoon, even though it was three days before the letters could be carried to the post. She told the story of how she came to be staying at the Manor house, instead of in Nanny Mallow's cottage. She did not wish to conceal the facts, not even the trick of fate that put her in a house with a woman just as close to her time as Linnet.

However, upon rereading her letter, Camilla was forced to recognize that she'd given rather less credit to Sir Philip for his generosity than he deserved. It was as if she was somehow reluctant to mention him. She did not feel as if she was ashamed of having been rescued by him; quite the contrary. Yet his name was only referred to in passing, and a cursory reading would do nothing to limit the impression that he was Lady LaCorte's husband rather than brother-in-law. She certainly never mentioned the story of the Paris wound. It would be much too hard to explain in a letter restricted to one sheet to hold down the cost of mailing it.

One week later, she wrote to impart the information that Dr. March thought it unwise for Nanny Mallow to return to her home, even with Camilla there to assist her. Sir Philip had insisted, therefore, that both Nanny and Camilla remain at the Manor for the length of Nanny's incapacity. She did not bring up the fact that young Grace had thereupon expressed the wish that Nanny's knee might never get better. Though Tinarose had reproved the little girl for speaking such an ill-wish aloud, she echoed it a day or two later.

"I wish you never had to go. It's comfortable having you here, Camilla."

"Why, thank you, Tinarose. You're very sweet."

The girl sighed. "I have noticed that it's not nearly so confusing now. We always know when tea is coming; before, it could come at any time between two o'clock and six. And we've had elevenses as early as nine and as late as at two."

"I hope elevenses at two and tea at two didn't happen often."

"Oh, that was all right. Then we'd hide a few cakes and things for later when we'd get hungry."

Camilla shook her head. "I hope I haven't interfered in the running of the house. That would be unforgivable in a guest."

Tinarose dropped her sewing into the workbox beside her and went to the morning room window. "I thought I heard a carriage," she said in explanation. Apparently, however, no one had come, for she turned away again with a sigh. She did not return to her patchwork but, putting her hands behind her, rocked idly against the edge of the piano. "No, you don't interfere," she said. "But everyone seems to want to please you."

"You know, I always thought it would be wonderful to have half a dozen servants waiting on you," Camilla said, smoothing a seam firmly. "When I would be washing the dishes or baking the bread, I'd think, 'Now the butler is coming to ask me if I'm at home to callers,' and I'd say, 'Tell Her Highness I shall be with her directly I scrub the tureen.' "

"Sometimes they are underfoot," Tinarose said. "I shouldn't ever like to be without them, though. How ever you manage with only a daily woman. . . ."

Camilla turned a hem over and adjusted a pin. "It's what I've always done, so I suppose I don't think of it, at least, not often. As my mother says, 'One makes a virtue of necessity.' "

"That's the sort of thing mothers always say."

"I dare say we'll be echoing it to our daughters one day and then blush to think how much we sound like our mothers." She held up the little dress she'd been fashioning from some white linen. "I hope I haven't made these sleeves too long. Nanny says not, but it looks more like a dress for an ape than a human child."

Tinarose came closer to look at the infant's dress. "It looks all right to me. You did compare it to some of the dresses we used for Grace, so it's bound to be all right. My, Grace was hard on clothing. You know she started to pull up on the furniture almost as soon as she could crawl. Once she took hold of a tablecloth and pulled a whole glass of red wine over on herself. She looked like Julius Caesar in the Senate."

"Gruesome," Camilla said, laughing.

"Yes, it was. I picked her up to carry her to our nurse, and she shook wine all over my favorite dress. There was nothing to do but dye it red. I was terribly upset."

"You have a red dress, Tinarose?" Camilla asked, remembering how she'd thought the younger girl would look splendid in brighter colors than the cold white or bland pink forced on her by fashion. "You should wear it."

"Heavens, Camilla! It was five years ago. Nelly has it now. It's so faded she uses it for her painting smock."

"You should make another."

"Mother would never hear of it. She hated that dress after we dyed it. She'd let me wear it only if we were sure not to have visitors." That apparently reminded her of her other preoccupation, for she turned again to the window.

Camilla hadn't been in the house three days before Tinarose had made her her confidante regarding her feelings for the handsome doctor. While searching for a piece of paper in the schoolroom to write her letter to her mother, she'd come across, quite accidentally, a page covered over with variations on the theme of "Mrs. Doctor Evelyn March."

She'd been very much surprised when Tinarose, coming up behind her, suddenly snatched the paper out of her hand, ripping it in two. Tinarose had stamped her foot, turned bright red, and burst into tears of embarrassment.

When Camilla neither scolded nor trotted off to tell but silently handed her a handkerchief, she made a friend for life.

"I know I'm a fool," Tinarose confessed now, going to sit down again in her chair. With a sigh, she picked up her abandoned patchwork. She had decided some months ago to make a new counterpane for her bed out of some old curtains, and matching the long green and white stripes kept her busy.

"Every girl is allowed one hopeless passion," Camilla said. "I've told you about mine."

"I hope I grow out of this one soon. He's so attractive, I know one day there'll be some girl who'll just snatch him up. I think I may be relieved when it happens."

"Very wise," Camilla said with a half smile. Then she heard the front door close solidly, and a familiar booted tread came along the hall. Hastily, Camilla tucked the baby dress into her workbasket and turned to face the door, wishing she had just one more instant to tidy her hair.

Sir Philip entered, his face flushed with the cold. He gave a smacking kiss to Tinarose. She squealed at the frigid touch of his cheek. "It's bracing," he admitted. "Chased the cobwebs out of my brains."

Turning toward Camilla, he tossed his greatcoat over the arm of a chair near the door, letting his hat fly to rest on top. "I've thought of a whole new way to end chapter four. He receives a message to meet Genevieve in the half-ruined chapel, but when he gets there, smugglers attempt to kidnap him."

"Why? Have they been bribed? By the evil landlord?"

"Remember, we made him a duke."

"That's right. So the duke bribed the smugglers?"

"To take him to the Crusade. He'd have a hard time getting back from there in time for the joust."

"You're both quite mad," Tinarose said. "But it does sound exciting, Uncle Philip. Will you let me read it, too?"

Camilla and Philip had both started in surprise when the girl spoke. A little concerned that they could so easily forget their duty to others when engaged in literary creation, Camilla picked up her sewing. Why had she been about to let it drop so carelessly? The dress might have become dusty when she'd thrown it down like that.

"Your mother doesn't approve of novels. I couldn't let you read it without her permission."

"That reminds me, Sir Philip," Camilla said with a great air of innocence as she continued stitching the hem. "Mavis was complaining that you leave your papers strewn about the library so she doesn't know what is to be kept and what needs to be thrown away or burnt. I don't blame her for being confused. I had to throw myself across chapter two yesterday for fear she'd start the fires with it."

"I'll try to do better," he vowed. "Perhaps if I left the completed chapters in my upper left-hand desk drawer?"

"That's a very good idea."

"I think so," he said, adding in a very stagy whisper, gesturing with his thumb toward the office, "It has a very secure lock. You can only open that one by pressing the key in as you turn it."

"Ingenious," Camilla exclaimed just as obviously. They neither of them peeked to see if any of this elaborate and blatant by-play had reached the target. She smiled up into Sir Philip's face as he sat above her on the arm of the chair.

Tinarose continued to look at them as if they'd lost their minds, instead of offering her a broad hint on how to circumvent her mother's unreasonable ban of novels, even that of Tinarose's own uncle's imaginings.

"What are you making?" he asked, touching the soft fabric.

"A little dress for your future niece or nephew. Tinarose said that Lady LaCorte hadn't the opportunity to make many new things." Crushed by the announcement of her husband's death, Lady La-Corte had put down the baby dress she'd been embroidering and had never picked it up again.

"Ah, that reminds me," Philip said, reaching for his greatcoat. "A letter was waiting for you at the inn."

"You rode so far?" Camilla asked, glancing at the window to see the weather.

"Icarus enjoys the snow, so long as it isn't actually falling, and we both needed the exercise. Besides, I had some urgent affairs to see to."

Camilla glanced curiously at Tinarose, who shrugged. What "urgent affairs" could have arisen between yesterday, a day that was no worse than today, and this morning? He'd received no letters; no messenger had arrived.

"Nothing serious, I trust?"

"It could prove to be exceedingly serious."

Tinarose grew alarmed. "I do hope it's nothing that will upset Mother. She seems happier today."

Camilla let the conversation go on without her as she looked at the carefully folded piece of paper. Her mother had found someone to frank her letter, and the date meant it had been only a few days in transit. Rising, she carried it over to a wastepaper basket in the corner and slid her finger under the seal, letting the crumbling wax fall neatly into the basket.

The first paragraph made her turn at once to her friends. "I'm an aunt," she chirped. "Linnet was safely delivered of a girl three days ago. They're calling her after me."

"Wonderful," Philip said. "Everyone all right?"

Camilla nodded, still reading. "Yes, all perfectly healthy. Except for my brother-in-law. He fainted upon hearing the news. Mother says he should be fully recovered by now."

"Why on earth would he faint?" Tinarose asked.

"Nervous prostration," Philip said wisely. "Your

father told me once he thought women had the easier share in childbed. It's the only time in his life, so he said, that he had no power over what would happen. He could only pace about the library waiting for the verdict."

"I'm sure he exaggerates," Camilla said, looking up.

"I don't think so. For a man to wait to hear whether his wife and child will survive, knowing he can do nothing to influence the outcome, must be mental torture of the most refined kind. I don't mind telling you that it is one of the things that has held me back from stepping into marriage."

Tinarose laughed. "Uncle Philip, you're a coward!"

"When it comes to matters of the heart, yes, I am. But I'm getting braver in my old age."

Camilla froze, knowing that if she should look up, she would find Philip's gaze fixed on her. Though he'd said nothing as yet, she'd begun to feel that his friendship for her had started to change. Sometimes, she was sure she must be the victim of her own too-vivid imagination. Other times, she felt sure it was only her comparatively unprotected state that kept him from seizing her in his arms. Nor could she constrain the sudden thrill that filled every atom of her being at the thought of his acting so impetuously.

"What else does Mrs. Twainsbury say?" Tinarose asked. "It's a long letter just to announce a birth."

Camilla reined in her wild thoughts and focused on her mother's neat script. Despite the clarity of her hand, Camilla soon found herself frowning.

"Not . . . bad news?" Tinarose added.

Looking up, Camilla saw both her friends looking at her with mild alarm. "Oh, nothing of importance," she said, forcing a smile. Philip looked as if he wanted to question her further, but Mavis entered and bobbed a curtsey to find them all there.

"If you're none too busy, miss, her la'ship asks if you'd come up."

"Of course. Certainly. Tell her . . . I shall be with her directly." Camilla shook out the folds of the little dress. "Shall I press this, Tinarose, or give it to her now?"

"Oh, now, Camilla. It will cheer her up even more; it's so pretty. I'll take it and press it later."

She rapped gently on Lady LaCorte's chamber door. Despite having been in the house more than a week, she'd yet to cross this threshold. After a moment without reply, she hesitatingly turned the knob. She saw a pleasantly appointed room, the walls a mix of cream distemper and a green-striped wallpaper.

Though the colors were feminine, the furnishings were not. Of dark wood, massive posts heavily carved, the bed dominated one end of the room while a pair of immense wardrobes stood like sentinel towers against each wall. The gold-framed paintings were of naval battles, complete with cotton-wool smoke and heaving seas. A brass spyglass on a wooden easel stood by the window, throwing off gleams from the winter sun.

Beside this was a chaise, upholstered in a deep moss green velvet that matched the curtains. Lady LaCorte lay upon it, a book fallen upon the floor below her drooping hand. She looked as if she were asleep. Camilla prepared to shut the door.

"No, come in, Miss Twainsbury," the woman said without rousing.

"I don't wish to disturb you, ma'am."

"Oh, well . . ." Lady LaCorte moved her shoulders with a kind of restless discomfort. "I'm so sleepy these days. I'm not resting well at all. It's always so in the last weeks."

Though Camilla remembered perfectly the insult offered her sister when she'd first met Lady LaCorte, she decided to impart her good news. "My mother writes to inform me that my sister was safely delivered of a child last week."

"Indeed?" Lady LaCorte smiled. "You must be very pleased. What sex is it?"

"A girl, ma'am."

"Another girl . . . poor thing. There are too many of us as it is. I fear for our daughters, Miss Twainsbury. What is to become of them?"

"One may always be a spinster and keep house for more fortunate relations."

"But you would never settle for so menial an existence. I have observed you, Miss Twainsbury; you have gifts quite out of the common way."

"Not at all, ma'am. As for a menial existence, I have lived that very comfortably since my childhood. I can truss a bird, paint a room, scrub a floor, and sew a frock." With that, she handed Lady LaCorte the gift she'd held behind her back. Wrapped in a square of tissue and tied with a chance-met ribbon from Tinarose's sewing box, it looked mysterious and interesting.

With an effort, Lady LaCorte pushed herself into a more upright position. "What is this?" she asked, her gloomy eyes lightening.

"A little token of my thanks for your hospitality and kindness."

She found herself the recipient of a searching glance. "I believe you mean that," Lady LaCorte said, her long fingers smoothing the thin cloth wrapping.

"Of course."

"Won't you be seated, Miss Twainsbury?" She indicated a chair with a graceful gesture. "Bring it nearer."

She waited until Camilla was seated before she opened the gift. Her smile when she held up the little dress was all Camilla could have hoped for, tender with maternal dreams. "What fine stitches," she said, looking more closely.

"I hope I made it the right size. I guessed by Grace's old clothes."

"It will suit. I only hope . . ." She let her other hand rest a moment on the rise of her abdomen. Camilla couldn't help but notice that her hostess looked noticeably larger than she had at breakfast but was too well-bred to speak about it.

"Would you care for some water, Lady LaCorte? Or anything?"

"No, thank you, child. I am to have a glass of my cordial before long. So you've had a letter from your mother, then?"

"Yes. She wrote to me almost immediately."

"And all went well?"

"Apparently so. Furthermore, she writes that she feels she need not stay more than another week or so. The nurse has proven to have a satisfactory grasp of her duties." She didn't mention that this was the second nurse and the third nursery maid. The first servants had been dismissed almost as soon as Mrs. Twainsbury arrived. "So you see, ma'am, I shall not have to impose upon you much longer."

"Imposition?" Lady LaCorte repeated as if her earlier hostility had been only a joke. "You've been an exemplary guest, helpful, courteous and unobtrusive. We shall miss you, Tinarose most of all."

"I like her very much."

"She's a dear child. I'm afraid I haven't been the most attentive parent of late. She feels the loss of her father keenly. When he was at home, they were all but inseparable."

Camilla nodded, remembering her own father so well. "I don't know that anything you could have done would help her. We each must find our own way through grief."

"You are very wise for one so young. I won't scruple to confess that when you first came among us, I was suspicious of your motives."

"Were you, ma'am?" Camilla said noncommittally. She recalled Sir Philip telling her how much Lady LaCorte dreaded the thought of losing her home to some interloping female.

"I believe you may remember how very rude I was to you?"

"No, I have no recollection of it at all."

Lady LaCorte laughed, pressing her hand against her side. "I know now that I was foolish to be so concerned. I thought you were another of those low, scheming creatures who besiege my poor brother-in-law."

"I'm not interested in his title."

"Oh, they buzzed about him even before he inherited here. There's something about very dark hair and those light eyes that draws the ladies like bees to honey. My husband was not so handsome, but he and I never wanted anyone else."

"I envy you that," Camilla said. "For all that has happened, I envy you the security of knowing that your husband loved you."

Lady LaCorte pressed her hand to her cheek, catching the sparkling tear. "Yes. I had that at any rate."

"I'm sorry, ma'am. I don't wish to overset you. That was tactless of me."

Lady LaCorte chuckled, despite the tears that still glittered in her eyes. "I wish some of my friends had half your tact. If you only knew how many dreadful letters and visitors I've received in the last several months. Condoling with me on the one hand, terrifying me with tales of miscarriages, still-births, and other horrors on the other. I'll never understand why women feel compelled to tell other women the worst sort of stories at a time like this."

Camilla could only look sympathetically. Bearing Tinarose's concern in mind, Camilla wanted to encourage her ladyship's lighter mood and not again cast her into the dismals.

"I don't mean to frighten you," Lady LaCorte said. "No doubt it will be different when your turn comes."

"I doubt it. Some of the women at home are dreadful gossips and pass along every tale they hear, proclaiming that they only speak as they do because 'I thought you would like to know. . . .' "

"That's it, exactly. They are all so eager to tell you, from motives of purest charity, of course, all those things you have fought so hard to drive from your thoughts. As if I needed to be reminded that sometimes dreadful things happen."

"Or as if I wanted to know that one of my beaus was seen at the Assembly with another young lady, far prettier and better dressed than I could ever hope to be. Not that they saw her themselves—no, it is invariably a secondhand report."

"Or the disaster happened to the sister of a cousin's old schoolmate. Yes, I know that one. Heaven preserve us from 'kind friends.' "

"Heaven preserve us from our 'own good,' " Camilla echoed with a shudder.

Lady LaCorte laughed again, more freely than

Camilla had ever heard her, though still tinged with bitterness. "My favorite is always 'I know you better than you know yourself,' usually as a preface to some piece of advice you'd not take if your soul depended upon it. I had a maiden aunt who was fond of that phrase. She also liked 'When I was your age.' Which we knew to be impossible. She could never have been younger than fifty-five, even when she was a babe in arms."

"We?" Camilla asked.

"I have three sisters and two brothers. We are scattered to the winds, these days. My younger brother emigrated to America, two sisters married attorneys, another teaches school in Winchelsea, and my older brother is a gentleman farmer in the north. He was always my favorite. If . . . If by some miracle, this child should prove to be a boy, I want to name him after Tom."

"An excellent name."

"I think so. Although I loved my husband dearly, I never cared much for the name Myron. It's Greek, of course. So is Philip. I think his father was fond of Ancient Greece."

"He must have anticipated the modern madness for anything that smacks of ancient glories."

"When Myron and I first came to this house, there were the most dreadful copies of Greco-Roman statues in every corner and cranny. Over the years, I have arranged their disposal. I remember I gave one to old Dr. March. I believe he set it up in his back garden. It's all right for him. He's used to looking at naked torsos."

They went on talking, laughter coming more often and more easily as the minutes slipped past. Though Camilla never ceased calling her formally as ma'am or Lady LaCorte, and the older woman never forgot Camilla's innocence, they found much common ground in their shared sense of the ridiculous and absurd. Yet, despite her unexpected enjoyment of Lady LaCorte's company, Camilla was prey to the curious sense that Lady LaCorte was holding something back.

When Mavis came in to give Lady LaCorte her strengthening cordial, both ladies blinked in surprise at the carriage clock on the mantelpiece. "It can't be time for that yet!" Lady LaCorte said in protest.

"Yes, my lady. Regular as clockwork."

Mavis gave her mistress a small wineglass filled halfway with water, then a small brown bottle. Lady LaCorte tipped some purple-brown liquid into the glass and, giving back the bottle, stirred the mixture with a glass rod.

"Vile stuff," she said. Grimacing, she tossed it off with the ease of a dedicated toper; then her expression grew even more squeezed as if she'd bitten into a lemon or tasted alum.

"Thank heavens it's only twice a day." She sighed heavily and resumed her easy position on the chaise, her legs out in front of her, her back against the velvet-covered back.

"I should go and let you rest. What Dr. March will think of me for chattering at you for so long."

"No, wait a moment. Thank you, Mavis. That will do."

When the door closed behind the little maid, Lady LaCorte took a firm grip on Camilla's wrist. "Please be so good, Miss Twainsbury, to open that door, to see if she's listening," Lady LaCorte said in an urgent undertone.

"Why should she?" Camilla asked.

The tug on her arm spoke of desperation. "Go see."

More curious than concerned, Camilla did as

she asked and reported back smartly. "Not a mob-cap to be seen," she said.

"Good. Sit down. Miss Twainsbury, I'm most reluctant to bring this up now. . . ."

Camilla sat down and leaned close to catch the hurrying words that tumbled out. "If something isn't done very soon, not only will the children have almost no gifts, but the servants, too, will go away from Christmas empty-handed." She stopped, swallowed as if the next words took great effort. "If you could see a way to possibly help me, Miss Twainsbury?"

"Of course," Camilla said, reassuringly patting her hand. "Whatever you want to do, let me know. I'll be more than glad to assist in any way possible."

"You really are a very good creature. I'm determined, you see, not to let my husband's . . . absence . . . interfere with our usual holiday festivities. But, alas, in my present state, I can hardly tiptoe lightly into the attics for that special box or scramble up and down ladders arranging the holly and the ivy. If you will be my mobility, Miss Twainsbury, I believe I can give my children the kind of Christmas-tide I wish to give them."

Camilla felt certain that it had cost Lady LaCorte to thus approach a girl she did not care for in order to ask a favor. Aware of Lady LaCorte's jealousy, Camilla felt the only answer was to reiterate what had already been said. "I will do whatever I can to make Christmas at the Manor into an absolute delight. You have my word on that, Lady LaCorte."

CHAPTER ELEVEN

In the late afternoon, with the golden light of a clear winter's day sifting through the library curtains, Philip paced before the windows. As he came to each turn, he shot an anxious glance at Camilla's bent head as she sat on the sofa, reading. In a burst of white-hot creativity, he'd written an entire chapter in one night. His right hand still felt cramped, and the pages, ill-spelled and ink-spattered, showed the effort. Also, his head ached from frustration.

All day, he'd attempted to steal half an hour of Camilla's time, longing to hear her opinion of what he'd done. Yet she always seemed too busy to draw aside. Ever since she'd spent an hour closeted with Beulah two days before, she'd been scurrying about like a home-loving mouse, up attic and down cellar, whispering the corner with Tinarose or one of the other two children. When she wasn't afoot on some errand, she was sitting, her hands full of busywork, with Nanny Mallow. Finally, he'd cornered her by promising her an uninterrupted tea. Uninterrupted, that was, by everybody but himself.

Though he paused, hardly breathing, when she laughed and tried to peek when she made a pencil mark on a page, he was distracted from her reaction to what she read by the unexpected charm of her appearance. Something had changed her in just the two weeks since she'd come.

He remembered thinking when he'd first met her that she was rather ordinary, except for her eyes. Her hair had been scraped back from her forehead, and her clothes had hung upon her. Yet more had changed than just her softer hair and a more refined fit. Perhaps she'd gained a little weight. Certainly her cheeks were no longer as pale as wax. Yet none of these satisfied his curiosity. Something else had changed her. Or perhaps the change was within himself. Certainly she now seemed one of the handsomest girls he'd ever seen.

At last, she turned over the last page of manuscript and straightened with a sigh.

Philip, alive to every nuance of her behavior, came to pour her out a fresh cup. "That did not sound like the sigh of a girl enchanted by a tender love scene," he said. "Please correct me if I am wrong."

"Oh, no," she said brightly. "It was very romantic, indeed. The way he leapt over the garden wall to assure her that he still loves her despite everything was very affecting."

"Camilla," he said in his deepest tone, "tell the truth. I'm an author; I can stand it."

She raised her hands as if to disavow responsibility. "Come now, Sir Philip. I'm no critic."

He laughed. "This from the girl who told me to my face that my characters, wholly imaginary beings created from my own head, wouldn't possibly behave as I had written. Not to mention the girl who insisted that I rewrite half a chapter to save the family dog from a very pathetic fate."

"Too pathetic . . . ," she murmured, showing the dimple that only appeared when she knew she was being wicked.

"Aha! No critic, indeed." He handed her a teacup, prepared with half a spoon of sugar and no more than a drop of milk just as she liked it. "Go on," he urged again after she'd taken a sip. "What's wrong?"

"Nothing. I swear it. Only . . ."

"Yes? You know how I value your judgment."

This time, she sighed in resignation. "I don't know quite . . . It's no more than the smallest ghost of a feeling. I hardly know how to express it."

He waited for her to resolve her doubts, delighting his eyes with the way one lock of hair fell from the upswept coiffure to touch her cheek and the base of her throat. She wore a pearl gray round gown, one of her own, with an open collar rising only in the back so that all of the smooth column of her neck showed. Her skin was as white as a Grecian goddess carved in marble, but her warmth suffused the marble with rose. Philip made a mental note to describe his heroine that way, which did not diminish how he felt about Camilla. He'd already noticed certain traits of hers transferring themselves to his fictional creation.

Then she spoke. "I feel as if, for all Lucien's pretty speeches, he's holding back."

"Holding back?" he prompted when she paused again.

"No, that's not it," she said hesitatingly. "It's as if there's a certain calculation that influences all his actions and speeches. I feel as if he doesn't mean what he says in a deeper way, as if he's only speaking of his love to persuade her not to betray him. Oh, I'm putting this very badly."

"No, no. I understand what you mean, I think. How can I improve it, do you think?" He smoothed his hair. "It's not easy to put sincerity on a page with black ink," he said. "Shall I fill my bottle with purple, do you think?"

"No, Sir Philip," she said with some relief in her tone. "Your handwriting is difficult enough."

He picked up the ink-daubed pages and rifled through them. "I shall reread it myself. Perhaps that will show me how to improve it."

Camilla seemed about to speak but turned away.

"Camilla. . . ," he began, tossing down the pages and following her. "What else?"

"Nothing. Do you think we'll be able to go riding again tomorrow? I need the exercise, and I hope to find a few necessities in the village."

"Camilla?"

She would not turn toward him, still concealing her eyes, those talkative eyes. Philip touched her hand as he'd done before. Yet, suddenly, it wasn't enough. He wanted his arm about her waist, her body turning toward his, his hand on her cheek to bring her lips under his. But it would be unseemly, improper, and the most natural thing in the world.

Before he could either conquer his need for her or surrender to it, she was returning the pressure of his fingers, though still with face averted. "I'm afraid. . . ."

"Ah, don't be."

"I think . . . I fear that this lack is not in Lucien. I think it may be in the author, Sir Philip."

"Don't you think you could stop calling me sir?" he said tenderly. "You have been Camilla to me now for days." He paused in the very instant of raising her hand to his lips. "What do you mean? You're afraid the lack is in me."

She nodded and let her fingers slip from his. Somehow that hurt him more than her words.

"Come and sit down," he said.

"No, I . . . I've said too much as it is. No doubt I am a fool with too much imagination. I should go. The children and I have some things to do together. I promised."

"No. Camilla, please." Philip motioned to the sofa. "Please sit down and just talk to me. About anything you like. Have you heard from your mother today? I saw there was a letter from her in the post Merridew collected." He wondered if Mrs. Twainsbury's letter had overset her. He wondered if he had, by some unconscious error caused by his exhaustion last night, written something in his chapter that she should not have read. He couldn't have mistakenly used her name in place of his heroine's? It was possible, considering how much he'd begun to identify one with the other.

"As a matter of fact, there was. She says that my little niece is of such a lusty disposition that she feels no qualms in cutting her visit short. She's very grateful to you for permitting me to stay at the Manor for so long."

"Grateful? It is we who should be grateful to her. It's difficult to imagine this house without you in it. I know Beulah feels the same way. You know that Tinarose does."

"I hope you will allow her to visit us. Mother is quite taken with her already, just from what I have written."

"You write to her about us?"

"Naturally. I have no wish to keep secrets from my mother." She looked away then, though she'd been giving him furtive glances once the subject changed from his emotional shortcomings. Instantly, Philip was agog to know what secrets she was keeping from Mrs. Twainsbury. He also wanted acutely to know what she'd written about him.

"Can you tell me now, do you think?" He sat

back in the deep corner of the sofa, obtaining a full view of her.

She sat curved in upon herself, as if the self-confidence that had been building in her day by day had all flown. Philip realized this was the difference he'd noticed. She neither gazed about her with an air of slightly affronted surprise as she had done at first, nor sat with lips tight and hands folded, too cowed to speak. It hurt him with quite a sharp pang to see her looking less strong than he knew her to be.

"I've told you I hardly know what I mean. It's a feeling, and one should not speak of feelings."

"Why not? They're the only things we truly own."

"But such matters are too intimate. My mother says—"

"Yes," he said, not wishing to hear another of Mrs. Twainsbury's aphorisms. The woman seemed to have made a perfect religion out of respectability and conformity, two altars at which he could never bring himself to worship for long. "I hoped we are close enough friends to talk about such things."

"I believe that we are . . . Philip. Very well." She folded her hands in her lap. "It seems to me that you hide your true self from everyone. I have heard often how kind and sympathetic you are and of your goodness to the people of Bishop's Halt and your dependents."

"But in reality I'm a monster of selfishness and depravity?" he asked. "You've guessed my secret!"

"Don't joke. It's as if you are playing the part of the good uncle and the kindly landlord when in reality you don't want to be here at all. You want to go back to your other life. I hear it in your voice whenever you speak of your travels."

"What other life?"

"The one you lived in America and Italy and Russia and . . . Paris."

"Paris?" he repeated, suddenly wary.

"Yes. Do you remember when Dr. March told that story about finding you wounded in Paris?"

"Evelyn always tells that story when he's had a drop too much. It doesn't mean anything."

"Someone hurt you. That means something. How could anyone want to hurt you?"

"What do you want to know, Camilla?" he asked gently. "All my past secrets? They're not very interesting, but I'm sure I can invent something. Tell me what tales you've been dreaming up. What do you think I am?"

"I think you are . . . ," she said a little more quickly, not stopping to weigh her words as she'd done before. But the caution ingrained in her by her mother still kept her from finishing her thought.

Philip moved from his corner of the sofa with a speed that took Camilla aback. Her eyes flew open in surprise. He cupped her face in his hands, marveling even then at the smooth purity of her complexion, moving his fingertips slightly to feel the softness of her cheeks. "Be bold, Camilla. Tell this fool what you think of him so he can return the compliment. Because I'm longing to say out loud what I think of you."

"I think someone hurt you. Now you don't believe in love and so can't write it," she said, then bit her lower lip, astounded by her own temerity.

"I'm sorry," Philip said. "But you're wrong." Then he kissed her.

At first, sheer surprise held her immobile. Then, a heartbeat later, Camilla didn't want to move, afraid he'd stop if she so much as lifted a hand. He might think she was trying to push him away. Philip's mouth on hers was warm and soft, his hands strong on her shoulders. She felt a strange flutter under her heart, like a cageful of butterflies had just opened, taking all her worries with them in their flight. Unable to bear the suspense, she reached out to flatten her hands against his flame-pattern waistcoat.

When Philip broke the kiss, retreating no farther than to rest his forehead against hers, he laughed, a little breathless himself. "Camilla . . ."

"Yes, Philip?" she whispered.

"Just so that there's no mistake about it later . . . Are you listening, dear?"

For a moment, her heart died as she was certain he was going to tell her this was a mistake, that he'd had no intention of kissing her, that he'd only surrendered to an uncontrollable impulse.

"I'm listening," she answered warily.

"Just so that we both understand completely . . . That was a proposal."

"Oh. Was it?"

"Shall I make it more formally?"

She couldn't answer, stunned by the wonder of a moment she'd never even dreamed of except in her most secret heart.

"Camilla, I adore you. You're the woman I've sought my whole life, in every corner of the world. I never thought you existed, and here you were within fifty miles of my family home the entire time. Please, please say you'll marry me."

He tilted her face so that she must look at him. Though he smiled tenderly, there was such earnest anxiety in his eyes that she couldn't bear to see it. Catching his hand, she pressed her cheek into his palm.

This instant, she felt, was the bridge between her past and her future. She'd never given her future much thought. She'd known she would live with her mother either for always or until one of her sometime suitors worked up the courage to propose. She never imagined a man like Philip would want her for his wife.

"Are you sure?" she asked, determined to be fair even when every instinct demanded that she seize this moment and accept before he could change his mind. "I have so many faults that you don't know."

"Faults? I've seen none, and you have been my close study now for more than two weeks."

"Oh, you don't know."

He drew her head down to his shoulder and, while holding one of her hands, put his other arm about her. "Tell me," he said with a laughter in his voice that sounded something close to tears. "Tell me these horrible flaws."

"Oh, I'm lazy," she said. One wouldn't think a muscular shoulder could be so comfortable. "I'd far rather read a book than do anything else. Often I forget to do my allotted tasks when there's an interesting book to finish."

"Grievous sins all. But how can I chide you for them when I'm guilty of the same myself? What else?"

"I'm so impatient."

"You?"

"It's true. I want all the good things to happen right away. I never can bear to wait for anything. Why, I was actually happy to be sent away before Christmas because I find it so difficult to wait for Christmas morning, even though I always know what my presents will be."

"What are they?"

"A book, some toilet water, a bunch of fruit to freshen my best hat, and a . . ." Her voice trailed off.

"What was that?"

"An undergarment," she said primly.

His laugh shook her, too, but she didn't mind. "I promise faithfully never to give you any of those things for Christmas. We shall have it written in our vows that none but frivolous gifts shall be allowed on Christmas and our birthdays. Apples of perpetual youth, crowns of wild olive, kissing-comfits; these shall we have. And speaking of kisses . . ."

The second time was sweeter than the first and the third sweeter still.

"I must write to your mother at once. You've told her about me?"

"Not very much," Camilla confessed. "I hardly knew what to say. I've told her that you have written several books."

"Good. What else?"

"That's all." She saw that he looked puzzled and slightly hurt. "I didn't want to tell her too much. She might not even have let me stay this long if she knew about you. I may have led her to believe certain things."

"What things, Camilla?"

"That you and Lady LaCorte were husband and wife."

He shook his head as if to clear it. "I beg your pardon?"

"Mother would never let me stay in a house where there is a single gentleman. The impropriety of it would shock her terribly." Camilla suddenly realized that cuddling with a man while completely alone with him in the middle of the afternoon would be just as much an affront to her mother's sensibilities. She tried to put a little space between her side and Philip's, but he didn't seem to want to let her go. A good sign, she thought, relaxing against his side. Perhaps he was not completely repelled by her dishonesty.

"Did you like it here so much?"

"I liked you," Camilla said, unable to look at him. "I liked you very much, from the start."

He gave a little crow of triumph. "I never would have guessed it, 'Miss Twainsbury.' So prim, so *nimini-pimini*, so proper."

"I'm surprised you gave me a second glance, sir, after coming to such a conclusion. I'll thank you to sit a little farther off."

"A gentleman never lets his first impression stand when subsequent meetings prove it to be false. I knew you weren't quite so old-maidish when you threw that snowball at me. And I'm quite comfortable where I am." He stole a quick kiss. To show she had no hard feelings where such thefts were concerned, she gave him another, rather slower.

"Oh, dear," she said somewhat drowsily a few minutes later. "I shall have to tell Lady LaCorte that we are betrothed."

"I'll do it."

"She won't approve, I'm afraid. I know her opinion of me will drop again to what it was when I first arrived. A 'low, scheming creature,' as she put it, out to trap you into matrimony."

"I shall soon explain that, my love. I'm trapping you, make no mistake."

"I'm sure she'll think you are far too good for me."

"Well, at least *she* doesn't think I'm a married man. How I'll explain that misunderstanding to your mother, I can't think."

"You write fiction; I'm sure you'll manage. But your sister-in-law doesn't like me."

"I believe you are mistaken."

"What, again?"

"You were wrong about my being unable to express my feelings," he said, expressing them again.

"True, though I'm still curious about Paris." She was only teasing, but he suddenly frowned. Not, she thought, at her, but at some memory. "Is it so difficult to talk about?"

He looked at her and smiled. "What lurid tale have you imagined, Camilla? Maybe you should write it down so we can use it in our next book."

" 'Our next book'?"

"You don't think I'm going to put my name alone on the title page, after you've done so much?"

There was only one way to thank him for his kindness. This time, however, when he came up for air, he put her gently away from him and moved back into the corner of the sofa.

"You sit in that corner, and I'll sit in mine," he said, holding his hands up before him like barriers. He looked at her warily. She put on her best meek expression. "You're not fooling me, you know."

"Who kissed whom?" she asked.

"We'll debate that later." Then, as she started for him, he allowed her only one small kiss. "I'm serious, now, Camilla. You stay over there. I've taken quite enough advantage of this situation. Anything more would be wrong of me. You are younger than I and an unprotected girl in this house."

"Yes, Philip," she said, already plotting to weaken his morality later. "What about Paris?"

"Heavens, you're a stubborn woman. Very well." He closed his eyes as if to summon his memory like a genie from a bottle. Camilla scooted ever so slightly closer to him. When some slight, betraying noise gave her away, she instantly froze, looking up with such innocence that Philip would have suspected her anyway.

"I was a spy," he said so simply that Camilla was sure she misunderstood him.

"I beg your pardon? Did you say 'a spy'?"

"Yes."

She knew he watched for her reaction. "For which side?"

He laughed as if every word she spoke delighted him. "For ours, of course. I'd been working in France even before the Eagle fell. Then I went to Paris to report to the Duke of Wellington. Rumors were flying everywhere that Napoleon wasn't finished, that he'd rise again. Tracking those rumors down took all our time. As for the famous stabbing, that was thanks to a woman I never should have turned my back on."

"A woman? Was she pretty?"

"Thank God," he said. "I was starting to think you were more than human, Camilla. You restore my faith in the essential qualities of womanhood. No. She wasn't pretty. She was roughly fifty, had been through a revolution, an empire, and a restoration, invariably picking the wrong side to pin her faith upon. Though I escaped with important information about who was channeling money to Elba, she did manage to stick me like a pig. Bleeding buckets of gore, I made my way to Eve's doorstep, when he proceeded to trip over me. He's been dining out on that story ever since."

"He shouldn't. It could be dangerous for you." She grasped his hand nervously.

"I assure you there are no emperors or their minions hiding in the snowdrifts, awaiting their revenge. I did my duty in the best way I could and left with a huge sigh of relief at the end of the war." He took a deep breath and let it out. "It feels good to tell you," he mused. "The only other one I've told is Myron so that he wouldn't think his brother an utter wastrel."

"He wouldn't have thought that."

"Why not? I have never claimed to be anything very outside the ordinary. I am content now to just write my books and watch my flowers grow. What say you, flower? How much do you care to grow?"

Somehow, without either of them willing it particularly, they gave up their places, cold and so far apart, to cuddle closer together. Philip smoothed back the one errant lock of hair, marveling again that she'd given him a right to such intimacies. "I'll write your mother at once," he declared. "Will she accept me, you think?"

"Yes, once she meets you. But write also, by all means. I am underage, Philip. I must have her consent."

"I feel confident she'll give that. Without wishing to seem conceited, I'm quite the catch."

"I don't know," Camilla said, rising to her feet. He was quite right; they'd been alone together long enough to set tongues wagging. On the threshold, she turned back, a teasing twinkle in her eyes. "Mother always thought I should have at least a viscount."

CHAPTER TWELVE

Dreading the moment when Lady LaCorte would discover her perfidy, Camilla couldn't help but be relieved when her ladyship did not come down to dinner. Nanny Mallow, up but still favoring her injured leg, called to Camilla as she started downstairs.

"My, but you do look pretty," she said. "Such a color in your cheeks, as a young girl ought to have."

"Fine feathers," Camilla said, smoothing the long sleeve of her only dinner dress, a rich tobacco brown poplin.

"Is that all?" Nanny asked with one of her funny wise looks.

"No, Nanny."

"Sir Philip?"

"Yes, Nanny," Camilla said, feeling a kind of shy triumph.

Nanny gave a little crow of pleasure. "There now! If that's not just what I've been saying all along. When two people are meant to be matched, they're meant, that's all." She embraced the girl, patting her back. "And won't your mother be pleased when she comes? Such a fine young man, with everything handsome about him."

"I hope Mother will like him."

"She won't be able to help herself, mark m'words. She's too sensible a woman to whistle such a catch down the wind."

"I don't know. She's proud and might not like my marrying into such a wealthy family. I haven't any dowry or expectations, and my connections are not—"

"Pooh!" Nanny said emphatically. "If Sir Philip don't care for that, why should anyone? It's yourself he's marrying, and so he'll tell you himself."

Camilla felt comforted by the very act of telling someone her fears. Nanny Mallow was such a sensible, down-to-earth sort. She'd soon sift Camilla's fears into chimeras and brass tacks. The first she could dismiss for a while; the second she must deal with as soon as she could.

"I know one thing, Nanny. Lady LaCorte won't like this news."

"That she won't."

"She doesn't think very highly of me now. I can just imagine how she'll feel when she discovers this. She thought I came to entrap Sir Philip into marriage. I believe she had begun to change her mind, but this engagement will just confirm her prior opinion. I couldn't bear it if Philip broke with her because he wants to marry me."

"Don't borrow trouble," Nanny counseled. "Besides which, she's keeping to her room tonight. I took a good look at her, and I'm thinking she's coming near her time."

"Goodness! We should send for Dr. March."

"Not yet," she said, calming Camilla. "It's not time just yet, or I don't know my business. And if I'm wrong about it, I know more about bringing

children into this world than he ever will. Her la'ship
herself said she was glad I'm under her roof for
this very reason. She might not have sent for me 'special, but since I'm here, she'll make use of me."

"I'm glad you're here, Nanny. Imagine if she
needed help in the middle of the night and only I
were here."

"Then you'd send the footman hotfoot for me
even before you'd sent for Dr. March. But I am
here and already begun. I told her straight out to
leave off those nasty stays she's been wearing, and
she did."

"Oh, I thought she looked . . . bigger."

"I don't hold with wearing stays when you're expecting. I'm an old hen, and I think the old ways
are the best ways. It's not as if she were some fashionable highly finished piece of nature on the
strut in London. As a mother, she should be thinking about her baby, not the size of her waist."
Nanny Mallow developed this theme for some little time before catching a glimpse of the clock in
her room. "Hurry down, child. Whatever will Sir
Philip think of you, making him wait for his supper?"

What Philip thought of her was shown by the
gleam in his eyes and the way he conveyed her
hand up for a gentle kiss when she entered the
room.

On the other side of the drawing room, Tinarose
took great interest in these new signs of affection.
With her mother's continuing indisposition, Tinarose had become accustomed to spending the
evenings with her uncle and Camilla as a matter of
propriety. Philip had seen immediately that it was
in Camilla's best interest not to be alone with him
every evening between dinner and retiring. Camilla
had rather thought that it didn't do Philip's repu-

tation any good to be alone with her, though tonight she would have liked best to have the chance to reiterate their sentiments of the afternoon.

Constant acquaintance with older people had rubbed off some of the shy gaucherie that Tinarose had previously shown. Camilla, used to making the best of little, had shown her two or three easy ways to dress her hair that had improved her too-square face, as well as making her pretty neck look swan-like and showing her more than slightly attractive ears. Despite knowing that Tinarose's affection for Dr. March was quite impossible, Camilla couldn't wait to see what he thought of these few alterations. Regrettably, the few times he'd come by, Camilla and Tinarose had been busy with their Christmas preparations for the little girls, and no one had told them he was there until after he had gone.

They sat down together on the sofa, while Philip poured them each a glass of sherry. "What is going on?" Tinarose whispered. "Are you . . . all right?"

"Yes, of course," Camilla said with a laughing glance at Philip.

He gave them their glasses and raised his high. "To Camilla," he said. "Who has graciously agreed to take on the arduous task of marrying me."

Tinarose squealed with delight, dropping her wine with the effect of having thrown it. She jumped up to embrace Philip. "I'm so glad," she cried.

He looked with comical helplessness over her shoulder as he patted her back. Camilla stood up. "I was afraid you wouldn't like it," she said.

"Not like it?" Tinarose turned quickly from Philip, gathering Camilla into a congratulatory embrace. "But when did this happen?"

"This afternoon," Camilla said, giving the girl a

kiss on the cheek and encouraging her to sit down again. "In the library."

"Oh," Tinarose sighed ecstatically. "It's so wonderful. When will you be married?"

"I hardly know. We must await my mother's consent."

"She'll give it; I know she will."

"I certainly hope so," Philip said, on his knees beside the miraculously unbroken stemmed glass, mopping with his handkerchief at the puddle of wine rapidly being absorbed into the rug. "Never mind," he said, seeing Tinarose's stricken look. "I dare say Samson will know how to remove it, and, failing him, who knows what wonders Nanny Mallow can perform? Wine must be the least of what she's removed from carpets, having been a child's nurse."

Tinarose ignored this. "Do you mean there's a chance Mrs. Twainsbury won't give consent? But surely . . . I mean, he has a title and money and this house and everything."

"You overwhelm me," Philip said, sitting back on his heels.

With a laughing look, Camilla shook her head at him. "Of course, I've considered all those things and have decided to accept him anyway. I'm sure Mother will have no difficulty approving as well."

"Oh, I do hope so. It would be just dreadful if she didn't."

"You're being very flattering," Camilla said.

"I mean it," Tinarose said, taking Camilla's hand in a friendly clasp. "You've been so good to me. Having you in the family will be like having the older sister I've always wanted. Besides, when you're a fashionable matron, just think what fun we'll have in Town when I make my come-out."

"Yes, we will. That is, if my lord and master permits me to go junketing about London." Camilla knew this was a light promise. A thousand things might prevent her from attending Tinarose in London, the most likely being that she might find herself in Lady LaCorte's condition. Looking speculatively at Philip, she caught his eye and suddenly was all one blush.

Though he asked her later why she'd colored, Camilla didn't tell him. She couldn't help but be a little shy when alone with him the next day, but since he seemed determined to press on with the book, she soon managed to put herself once more on an easy footing with him. Only, when at the end of an argument regarding a scene with the heroine was resolved, Philip kissed her cheek. Unable to meet his eyes, she put her hand up to touch the side of his face.

"Camilla," he said, holding her hand there. "You're not having second thoughts?"

"No, certainly not. It's just . . . Well, it's a little strange. I know you so well as my dear friend; it will take some little time to know you as my lover."

"Not too long, I trust? For I intend to be very ardent, you know. But you are right, oh, queen of common sense."

"What a horrible thing to be!"

"But you are a wonder of sense, Camilla, common and otherwise. I knew it from the first." He withdrew his arm from around her. "Though I wish I could spend every minute of the day with you, both as your lover and your collaborator, I think it's wisest if I take Dr. March up on his long-standing invitation to hold bachelor household with him and his father for a few days."

"Must you?" Camilla said, and he smiled.

"You'll miss me?"

"It just seems a shame when we were making so much progress on our book."

"Just our book?"

"Of course. To let you know that my life will be a barren desert until I see you again would lower me too much in your opinion."

"No, it wouldn't," he claimed, eagerly reaching for her.

"My mother has often told me to reveal less of my emotions than I feel so that no one might take advantage of a weak moment. And you know Nanny Mallow has also warned me that a woman must surrender no advantages when she marries, for the law takes away quite enough as it is."

"I hope they are mistaken," he said, more seriously. "I hope you won't ever pretend to me. I'm a greedy fellow and want to know the full depth of your feelings. But I'm not selfish. I have every intention of showing you just what you mean to me."

Camilla held out her hands to him, letting him see the tears that had come into her eyes. "I'm afraid, Philip."

"Afraid? Of what? If it's my constancy . . ." He folded her in his arms, laying her head on his shoulder, conscious only of the wish to protect her, to keep her safe from all hurts, even those he might, through carelessness or thoughtlessness, inflict.

"I don't know what I have done to deserve such happiness," she said softly. "I'm afraid whatever it was will prove to be too little and I will lose you."

"Never," he swore, knowing that others had sworn the same countless times only to be forsworn a day or an hour later. He tilted up her chin and kissed her trembling lips.

Therefore, Philip was not at the Manor when Mrs. Twainsbury arrived to take her daughter home. Camilla had been out for a walk with Tinarose and the two children. Coming down the now-cleared drive, bundled up to the eyes against the frigid afternoon air, Camilla saw a nice-sized chaise being driven off to the stable yard. "That must be Mother," she said.

"It's a handsome turnout," Tinarose said. "A coachman and a footman."

"They must be my brother-in-law's men. I didn't realize he'd started keeping his own carriage." Camilla began to hurry on, turning her haste into a game so that the little ones would hurry, too. She wished profoundly there had been time to tidy her hair and wash her face before meeting her mother, but their long separation brooked no delay.

"Camilla!" Mrs. Twainsbury said, holding out her arms. She did not embrace her daughter but held her off at arm's reach. "Let me look at you."

Though her bright smile never faltered, Camilla could tell by the gradual hardening of the brown eyes that she was not pleased by what she saw. Cold air may be bracing, but it was hard on the complexion, not to mention the stringy and matted hair occasioned by tight knitted hats.

"We went for a walk, Mama. It was stuffy in the house."

"Yes, too many fires, I'll be bound. Large rooms are so difficult to heat. And who is this?"

"Mama, may I present Miss Tinarose LaCorte. This is her home. She has been more than kind to me, a chance-met stranger."

"Don't believe her, ma'am. The kindness has been all on her side." Tinarose stood smiling, hand outstretched. Mrs. Twainsbury gave her two fingers to shake, obviously not pleased by the young woman's free-and-easy manner.

"I trust your mother is feeling better today,"

Mrs. Twainsbury said. "I did so wish to thank her for her goodness to Camilla. I can imagine nothing more devastating to a well-run household than the arrival of the unexpected guest. And to stay for so long is quite unconscionable. My only excuse is the press of family affairs made it quite impossible to collect Camilla before now. I hope she'll forgive Camilla's intrusion at such a—ahem—delicate time."

"If I may venture to speak for my mother, I think she found Camilla to be a great help. I know I did."

Mrs. Twainsbury returned no answer. She'd caught sight of the two younger girls. "And who are they?"

"My sisters, ma'am. Nell and Grace. Say how-do-you-do to Mrs. Twainsbury, girls." Two identical curtseys, two mumbled greetings, and they began to edge out of the room.

"They should be in their nursery," Mrs. Twainsbury said firmly. "When my girls were young, they were never permitted downstairs between the hours of nine o'clock in the morning and seven at night, except for half an hour at six-thirty."

"You let them stay up late?" Tinarose asked, trying to work out this schedule on her fingers.

"On the contrary. They went directly to bed after kissing me good night and wouldn't appear again until breakfast, taken in the kitchen. Children should be given the opportunity to improve themselves before being thrust upon adult society."

Tinarose smiled graciously. "I shall take them up to their nursery at once. I'm sure you and Camilla have a great deal to say to one another." As she turned to herd her sisters away, she rolled her eyes heavenward and made such a funny, distorted face that Camilla couldn't contain a small giggle. Under her mother's disapproving glare, the giggle fell like a popped balloon.

"Oh, dear, Grace, your shoestring is untied," Tinarose said exaggeratedly. Positioning the child beside Camilla, Tinarose muttered, "Your mother is a Tartar," as she knelt to tend the child's boot. "I'm sending for Uncle Philip at once."

"Please do," Camilla muttered, under the cover of a handkerchief wiped over her admittedly shiny face. "Would you mind asking Samson to send up some tea, dear?" Camilla asked aloud as Tinarose bowed herself and the children out of the room.

Mrs. Twainsbury cast a glance around her, taking in the slightly worn appearance of the well-loved furnishings. She wore her gray heather walking costume trimmed in black tape and looked as neat from her undisturbed hair to her brightly shining boots as if she'd just descended from heaven, rather than from a cramped chaise. "To give you the word without roundaboutation, I tell you this house reminds me of those shabby-genteel persons who occupied Rosemount the summer the Fusters went to Bath for Sir John's health."

"There's nothing shabby-genteel about them," Camilla answered back, feeling protective of the Manor and all those who dwelt within it. "As I wrote you, the family has recently undergone a loss which has made the day-to-day continuance of life very difficult. He was too good a man to lose, both personally and professionally."

"Your letters were the most uninformative scribbles I've ever had the misfortune to receive," Mrs. Twainsbury said with her light laugh. "This Sir Philip, for instance, sounds a flimsy sort of person to inherit such a large property."

"On the contrary, he's a man of considerable intelligence and kindliness." Camilla wondered what her mother's reaction would be to a sudden announcement that she'd fallen in love with him and he with her. Though she had no intention of announcing such a thing without him standing by her side to offer support, she felt a warm glow in her heart knowing that he loved her. She decided to gauge her mother's feelings without revealing the fact of their betrothal. It was obvious her mother hadn't yet received Philip's letter asking for her hand.

"What profession did he pursue prior to inheriting this property?" Mrs. Twainsbury asked, picking up a Sevrés vase from an attractively arranged table.

"Profession? He is an author, Mama, only fancy."

"A writer?" She tested the glaze with her fingertip, then set it down again, dusting her hands. "Published?"

"Yes. He has several books on traveling abroad presently in print."

"I see. He is a widely traveled gentleman, then?"

"He's been a great many fascinating places. America. The Hebrides. Greece and Italy. He is full of fascinating information about his journeys. Rather than just travel about, he took the opportunity to live amongst the citizenry, learning about their lives firsthand."

"It sounds thoroughly uncomfortable. I believe such places are exceedingly backward where proper drainage is concerned. However, I shall be most interested to hear what he has to say. He is a man of information, a scholar, then?"

"He understands a great many things, I believe. He explained the entire subject of the Irish Question so that a child might understand it." Camilla couldn't recall which college Philip had attended. He himself had said he had not done well there.

Mrs. Twainsbury, a great advocate for education, would undoubtedly take his lack of matriculation as a black mark against his name.

"I see. So he is from home at present?"

"Yes, Mama. He is visiting friends for a little while."

"I see. Now for more important matters . . . In her latest letter to me, Nanny Mallow suggests that Lady LaCorte is in the same interesting condition as your sister was. Is this true?"

"Quite true," Camilla said, apostrophizing herself as a fool not to have realized that Nanny would have seen no reason to cut off her lengthy correspondence with one of her former charges. But how much had she revealed? How had she managed to learn anything relevant, confined to her room for more than half the length of Camilla's visit? The servants, she supposed, must pass the long hours gossiping, and as Nanny Mallow wasn't gentry, there were no social barriers to stop them gossiping with her.

"Well, she's in good hands with Nanny Mallow," Mrs. Twainsbury said. "She may be elderly, but she is clean and well intentioned if rather sentimental."

"There's also a very competent doctor in the area," Camilla said. "That's where Sir Philip is now. He felt that remaining here might work some harm to my reputation, once Lady LaCorte discovered herself no longer able to descend for dinner."

"Quite right. He shows a nice feeling for propriety."

Though he'd always been a gentleman, somehow Camilla could not reconcile propriety and Philip. There was always too much happiness and a sense of possibility in his outlook to make decorum one of his household gods. She realized now that her mother, whatever she'd been in her youth, had lost both happiness and hope somewhere along the way.

She did not mention the other reason Philip had for leaving his home because it was too precious to be exposed to derision or disbelief. She knew he'd not left his home simply to stop people gossiping but because staying exposed them both to temptations too strong to be resisted. Remembering the desire in his eyes, feeling that longing echoing in her own heart, Camilla knew he was right to go. But she could hardly expect her mother to share in her joy over such a thing.

"I expect Sir Philip will return to greet me as is correct," Mrs. Twainsbury said.

"I believe that he will."

"Then kindly escort me to your chamber so that I may freshen myself, and you, Camilla, must tidy your appearance. We shall rest one night here so that you may have an opportunity to say your farewells and to rest the horses. Then we shall return home, departing not a moment later than nine o'clock."

"Yes, Mama." Camilla consoled herself for the abruptness of this departure by reminding herself that by tomorrow, her mother would be so exalted by the announcement of her daughter's betrothal that all thought of leaving would be banished from her memory.

When Philip arrived at the Manor, brought hotfoot by Tinarose's message to "waste no time," he felt as he had when once taken bear hunting in America. His guide hadn't known for certain whether there was a bear in the cave before him or not, but it had behooved them both to be cautious.

Samson met him at the door, ready to take his greatcoat and hat. "Miss Twainsbury and her mother are in the drawing room, Sir Philip."

"Everything all right?" Philip said in a rapid undertone as he stopped before the mirror.

"No, sir. Mavis brought in the tea. I beg your pardon, sir, for not attending to the matter myself. It did not occur to me that Mavis's manner would be a problem as Miss Twainsbury is such a pleasantly spoken young woman."

Philip smiled at the butler, a friend from his childhood. It meant a great deal to him that he should approve his master's choice of wife. "Yes, she is, isn't she? Well, it doesn't matter, Samson. Mrs. Twainsbury might as well know the worst of us at once. She stands on ceremony, I take it."

"As upon a rock, sir."

It took him only one glance to realize there was a bear in the cave after all. Mrs. Twainsbury greeted him pleasantly enough, but Camilla looked just as she had when he'd first met her in the coach. Her lips were pressed tightly together as if to keep back words by main force. Her hands, too, were strained together while her feet were tucked back under her chair almost to the point of having vanished. She wore the most unappealing of the dresses she'd brought with her instead of one of Beulah's borrowed gowns.

When he approached her to kiss her cheek, she gave the slightest shake of her head while her entire body retreated like a snail into its shell. He stopped abruptly. "Mama, may I present Sir Philip LaCorte."

If he'd been building an image in his mind of

an ogress, with a hard red face and a bosom that would do for an armed bulwark, he had to revise it. Mrs. Twainsbury held herself very much erect, yet even with her hair piled high, she could not have topped five feet by more than an inch or two. She was slender, with the narrow hands and feet of an aristocrat. Her fine drawn face bore few wrinkles except for the deep lines that ran from her nose to the corners of her mouth and the more delicate tracks of years about her eyes. Her evening dress, elegantly plain, could not have been more appropriate for dinner in the country.

When he approached and bowed, her greeting was correct. She smiled graciously and instantly engaged him in conversation about the severity of the weather. Yet Philip, sensitive to emotional atmosphere, realized two things about her. Firstly, she must have caught the scent of April and May in the air, for she was deferring pleasantly to his opinions and quite openly recommending her daughter to him.

Secondly, which roused all his chivalrous impulses, was that Camilla seemed genuinely frightened of the small, smiling creature in front of him.

Despite his wishes, etiquette demanded that he give Mrs. Twainsbury his arm into the salon. The two girls followed, Tinarose glaring openly at Mrs. Twainsbury's elegant back.

"I really must thank you and Lady LaCorte for all your kindnesses to my little girl, but I understand Lady LaCorte to be indisposed at present."

"It's very easy to be kind to Miss Twainsbury," he said, smiling through the candle flames at Camilla. She didn't see, keeping her eyes on her plate, though he noticed she only just tasted the food. "I must thank you for having the good sense to send her to Nanny Mallow's, else we might never have met."

"I must speak very strictly to Nanny Mallow," Mrs. Twainsbury said. "I don't like the thought of her being all alone here. If an accident may happen once, it may happen again with graver consequences. There is an almshouse for the care of aged menials not too far from our little village. I happen to know the director quite well. I am sure with a word from me, Nanny Mallow might have the next vacant bed."

"No, Mama," Camilla said, looking up at this. "Nanny Mallow would hate it there."

"Camilla, child, you interrupt."

"I beg your pardon, Mama," Camilla muttered to her plate.

Philip took a sip of cold water, hoping it would douse the flare of anger suddenly blazing in his chest. He would not begin his first acquaintance with his future mother-in-law by brangling. However, in the future, he'd have something to say to Mrs. Twainsbury on the subject of respecting one's child.

"As I was saying, it's a well-run institution. The elderly ladies are all set to some useful stitching, and the meals are regular. Best of all, Nanny Mallow need never be alone. The dormitory is visited regularly throughout the night by matrons so that nothing untoward may ever happen."

"Mama, I don't believe that Nanny Mallow wishes to give up her home and all her possessions in order to be sleeping in a drafty room with twenty other women. I remember visiting that place with you. Everything was run by bells. Up with a bell, eat with a bell, bed by a bell. Nanny Mallow would be miserable."

"It does sound dreadful," Tinarose said.

"Discipline is necessary at every stage of life. Young girls frequently cannot see where a person's best interest lies. Were Nanny Mallow at the almshouse, I should be able to visit her frequently to assure myself of her continued health."

"There's no need for that," Philip said. "I intend to interest myself in Nanny Mallow's continued good health. I have already given instructions for one of my servants to visit her daily, once she can return to her home."

"Don't send that Mavis creature," Mrs. Twainsbury said with a sharp smile. "She'd drive any sane woman mad in a week."

"She needs a trifle more training, perhaps," Philip conceded. "But we are all very fond of her." Under the table, he gave a sign for Samson to send Mavis's sister, serving tonight, out of the room. She went, leaving a growl behind her.

Philip did not stay for brandy after dinner, however badly he needed one, but accompanied his lady guests into the drawing room. Mrs. Twainsbury settled herself comfortably and called Tinarose to her side. "Camilla, I trust you haven't been neglecting your music while you are here. That looks a very fine instrument. Play for me."

"Very well, Mama," Camilla said. Though she gave him a strong indication not to seek a private moment, Philip joined her by the piano as she sought through the manuscripts in the bench.

"What's wrong, Camilla?" he said softly. "Why didn't you want me to kiss you?"

"Mother wouldn't understand."

"Why not? We're to be married."

"Here's one I know," she said brightly, pulling out a sonata. "She doesn't know that," she added hoarsely. "I haven't told her yet."

"Didn't she receive my letter?" He spread open the book. "I'll turn for you if you like."

"No. And there hasn't been a good opportunity for me to tell her. I'll do it tonight, when I go in to wish her pleasant dreams." She smiled brightly at him, her eyes haunted. "When I nod?"

"Let me tell her, Camilla. Whatever you're afraid she'll do, she can't do it in front of me. Even if she does enact me a scene, I shan't be impressed. I'd rather we were married with her blessing, but I'll marry you without it if I must."

"You forget," she said, starting to play. "I need her consent. Even if there were no other reasons, I must have her approval before I'll marry anyone."

"Oh, she'll grant it."

"Braggart," she said with a flash of the first genuine smile he'd seen from her all evening. If he hadn't already been in love with her, the acknowledgment of how cold he felt without her smile warming him would have given him the hint, just as his desire to warm her and keep her safe had informed him of his feelings the day they'd all gone sledding.

"Concentration, my dear one," Mrs. Twainsbury trilled from the sofa as Camilla's fingers faltered. "I'm afraid you haven't practiced very much at all, but still how delightful. Camilla's sister, Linnet, plays also but not just lately. Linnet has a more delicate touch upon the keys, but Camilla's gifts are accuracy and speed."

But there was to be no quiet talk that night. Camilla had reached an exquisitely slow and romantic passage when rapid footsteps approached the drawing room door. "Ah, that will be tea," Mrs. Twainsbury sighed, sitting up expectantly.

But Samson bore no tray. He approached his

master, his round face pale and sweating. "It's begun, Master Philip. I've sent Merridew to fetch Dr. March. Nanny Mallow is with her now, sir."

"What's that?" Mrs. Twainsbury demanded.

"Lady LaCorte's going to have her baby," Camilla said with a joy not even her mother's glance could quell.

"Oh, no," Tinarose said, pressing her hands together as if to pray. "Remember you said you'd sleep in the nursery if the baby came at night."

"I remember. We'll go up now. The little girls will be worried." She turned toward Philip and gave him her hand. "Tomorrow," she said with special intensity. "Without fail."

"Without fail." Seeing that she would prefer no other sign of affection, he gave her hand a gentle squeeze which should have communicated all his feelings. But perhaps, he reflected later, that was too much to ask of any simple gesture. Her eyes spoke so much more clearly.

CHAPTER THIRTEEN

Dr. March arrived within the hour, limping a little as he came up the stairs. Camilla and Tinarose were watching him from the next flight up and saw him shake hands with Philip. "Thanks to your riding lessons," he said, "I'm here in one piece, but, damnation, I wish you'd shown me the gallop. I'm shaken to bits."

"A brandy, then?"

"Thanks, no. Not the sort of thing you want on your breath while delivering a baby. Keep it warm for me, though, for afterward. I'll need it."

"You anticipate difficulties?"

"She is nearly forty, you know. But I'm sure between myself and Nanny Mallow, all will be well."

Philip sighed. "I only wish my brother were here. He had plenty of experience at this damned waiting."

Dr. March clapped him on the shoulder and went into Lady LaCorte's bedchamber.

Camilla had to all but pry Tinarose's fingers off the balustrade supports. "What shall I do if anything happens to Mother?" she asked.

"Don't worry. All will be well. It's not as if she's never had a baby before." Camilla continued talking soothingly to her friend as she helped her rise. Telling her not to let her sisters see her concern seemed the best way to steady her nerves. By the time she sat down to help them with their dolls, she had herself in hand.

Camilla wanted to slip out in search of Philip, but having promised to see Tinarose through these difficult hours, she didn't feel she could leave the nursery. However, after half an hour of pacing, of picking up books only to toss them aside, Tinarose took her a little apart from the others. "Go see Uncle Philip, Camilla. I'll stay here."

"Are you sure?"

She nodded. "I'm worried but not panicked. Come back as soon as you know anything, will you?"

When she entered the library, Philip gave her the tender smile that he seemed to keep for her alone. His cravat hung loose while his hair showed every sign of having been roughly handled. "How are the girls?"

"Tinarose is nervous, but the younger girls don't seem to be worried. They are too excited about having a baby in the house to think of anything else."

"And how are you?" He drew her to his side in the shadows between the lights of two candles.

"Happy. I think she liked you. She wouldn't have spoken so kindly about you if she hadn't."

With gentle fingers, he tilted her face so the candlelight fell on it. She tried to smile, but her lips trembled. "Camilla, dearest, can you tell me, do you think, why she frightens you so?"

"She . . . She doesn't. Of course she doesn't. She's my mother."

"But ever since she entered this house, you've

been so different," he said, his voice so warm with concern and love that she felt her heart turn to melted butter. "You don't smile; you don't laugh; you've hardly uttered a word beyond common politeness. I can't imagine why. Nothing has changed between us, unless I've hurt you in some way. If that's the case, pray tell me so. I'll make it right, Camilla."

She caught his hand and kissed it, leaving a smear of ink against her lower lip. "Not that. I am still of the same mind and know that I always shall be."

"Then why . . . ?" He pressed his lips to her temple. "Why such a change in you?"

"It's true I am not so prone to talk in my mother's company, but that is less her doing than yours."

"Mine?"

"I have been spoiled here at the Manor, I think. From the first, you have laughed at my jokes—a very heady experience. Before, whenever I spoke with jocularity, people would ask me what I meant. You never have."

She reached up and smoothed his tousled hair. "You have never seemed to find anything strange in my outspokenness, and so, I began to indulge my liberty to be more and more conversational."

"Then continue to do so, Camilla. You have every right to express yourself with whatever freedom you wish. Especially," he said softly, "when expressing your feelings for me."

He caressed her lower lip with his thumb, wiping away some of the ink. Her eyes drifted closed, and she rose up slightly, seeking his kiss. As with her words, he didn't seem appalled by any boldness on her part but accepted her affections with a joy that made her feel whole.

"Are you certain you don't want me to tell her? I can be diplomatic about it."

Camilla laughed, the softly intimate laughter of a lover. "You're a brave man, Philip, but that's too great a task for even a knight in invincible armor to undertake to prove his love. I'll go now, shall I?"

"No," he said huskily, drawing her closer yet. "Not just now. I've been three days without the taste of you, and I'm not letting go so soon."

Sometime later, adjusting her hair before a mirror, Camilla noticed her softly swollen lips and the bemused expression in her eyes. Her mother was no fool. As soon as she laid eyes on her, Mrs. Twainsbury would know what Camilla had been doing.

Philip escorted her to her room which Mrs. Twainsbury had suggested they share for this last night under the Manor roof. He smiled down into her eyes. "You blush more becomingly than any woman I've ever seen. To say your cheeks are like pink roses may be a cliché, but I'm dashed if it isn't true."

"Hush," she said, for he'd spoken in normal tones. She glanced toward her own door while Philip looked down the hall.

"I'm glad you're sleeping in the nursery tonight. This floor is apt to be bustling all night."

Now Camilla looked toward Lady LaCorte's chamber. "I shall," she said. "But first . . ." She laid her hand on her doorknob. "Good night, my love. I shall be first down to breakfast tomorrow to tell you what has occurred."

"I'm not tired," he said, laying his hand over hers so that she could not turn the knob yet to leave him. "Come back to the library as soon as you have the word. I'll be there until Evelyn comes down with the news of what he's brought into this world."

"If it's a boy . . ."

"Can you bear to marry an ordinary 'mister'?"

"Whatever you'll be, it won't be ordinary." She received a swift kiss for that. "If I can come down again, I shall."

"I can't ask for more than that. 'Til then."

Camilla waited until he was out of sight before she entered. Mrs. Twainsbury bustled about in the midst of Camilla's clothing, borrowed and personal. "Ah, there you are. What news of Lady LaCorte?"

"Nothing yet, Mama." She picked up a pair of stout leather shoes and put them back in the wardrobe. "Those aren't mine. Neither is that pink Indian muslin."

"Are you certain?" Mrs. Twainsbury asked, holding up the thin nightdress. "To be sure, you had nothing in such a color when you left, but laundresses are so careless. They can't seem to be taught not to mix other colors with white."

"No, Mama. It's something Lady LaCorte lent me. She's been so kind. Everyone has been so kind. Especially Philip."

"Sir Philip," her mother corrected. "Remember it's vulgar to call people by their first names unless they are particularly well known to you and have asked you to do so. Salting a conversation with the personal names of public or exalted figures is nothing more than fraud since it indicates a closer relationship than exists. Just because you have been on terms of some intimacy these last few weeks is no reason to drop the barriers of propriety. I'm sure he doesn't call you Camilla behind your back."

"He has asked me to call him Philip, Mama, and I hope he will always wish to call me by my name." Though her mother was frowning at her, usually enough to set her a-quake, Camilla was still buoyed up from Philip's evident admiration and love, as well as from his remarkably effective kisses. She felt a sudden ripple of joy from somewhere under her ribs at the memory, as if her heart danced.

"I hope you have not passed the line of what is pleasing," Mrs. Twainsbury said, folding Camilla's own nightdress with crisp little jerks. "Gentlemen are not to be trusted with young ladies fresh from the schoolroom."

"I know I can trust Philip to protect me even from myself," Camilla said in a defiant whisper, hoping she'd not be called upon to defend that statement with charts and graphs. "As for propriety, Mama, as you know, Philip has removed to Dr. March's house while the Manor has no mistress capable of her duties. His designs toward me are entirely honorable. In short, he's asked me to be his wife."

"I beg your pardon?" Mrs. Twainsbury blinked as if she honestly hadn't heard a word.

"Philip loves me and wants to marry me. I have accepted him." Camilla breathed again. There, she'd gotten all of her message out without resorting, as she had feared, to mime to cover her tongue-tiedness.

Mrs. Twainsbury sat down on the bed, a clear infringement of her tribal laws. "I—I can't fathom it," she said. "You're sure it's marriage he's offered?"

"He's too much of a gentleman to have offered anything irregular." Camilla felt the tension leave her neck and shoulders. Strange to say, it had been harder to dread the telling than to tell it. "I hope we may hear that you approve of this step, Mama."

"Approve?" Mrs. Twainsbury appeared to be thinking of something else. "I never would have thought it of you of all people, Camilla."

Worried again, Camilla spoke more quickly. "I

realize he should have asked you properly for my hand, but it really has only been a very few days since the subject first arose. He's such a *good* man, Mama. If only you could know him better, I'm sure you'd think so, too."

"Of course, fate played a considerable part in this. You couldn't have orchestrated Nanny's accident; 'twould be wrong, and you were miles away when it occurred. Yet to take such swift advantage of the situation in which you found yourself was really a stroke of genius that I had never expected lay within you. I never took you for such a downy one, Camilla."

Downy? Genius? These were not terms her mother had ever used for her. Her adjectives were "bluestocking" and "Miss Clever" usually prefaced by "Don't be such a. . . ."

"Who told you that the LaCorte fortune had passed to the younger son? And what a fortune! Sir Myron lived on his pay and prize money, but I've heard that they might have in the Bank of England as much as a hundred thousand pounds. A hundred thousand . . . yes." She looked about her incredulously. "Yet they live with old pictures and old wallpaper in all their rooms. Even this coverlet is only silk on one side."

"I don't know anything about that," Camilla said, wondering if she should fetch a vinaigrette or some hartshorn. Her mother seemed to be wandering a little in her thoughts. "Then you do approve, Mama?"

"Had you this plot in mind when you submitted with such a good grace to my sending you to Nanny's? If I had but realized that Sir Philip was at home, I could have sent you here months ago. Heavens, you could already be settled as a LaCorte today. Well, there's no use in repining over lost opportunities so long as you leap upon the next one."

"Mama," Camilla said, narrowing her eyes. "Are you saying that you think I—I set my cap for Sir Philip because he's wealthy?"

"Of course, it would never do to admit such a thing outside of these walls." She clasped her hands together and raised her eyes ecstatically toward heaven. "I thought I did well to marry your sister off so creditably. When your brother-in-law offered for Linnet, I counted it a personal triumph. Sir John Fuster's son was the height of my ambition for you, you know. You both being so very blue. But this! My dear child, you may well find yourself presented at Court."

"I hadn't given that any thought."

"No, how should you? You've had quite enough to plan here." She laughed and rose. Embracing her daughter about the shoulders, she kissed her. "Now you must be cautious. Be advised by me."

"Mama, I assure you that I did not chase Philip. I never thought about money or title in connection with him. He is the man I love, so greatly, so completely. I should love him if he were a pauper." Her voice quavered under the stress of her feelings, but her mother didn't seem to understand.

"Very wise of you to say so, my dear. There's nothing more distasteful than an openly mercenary young girl."

"But it's true."

Mrs. Twainsbury gave her light laugh. "Let us hope you need never be put to the test. Marry him if he were a pauper—as if I should ever permit that. No, my dear. Disguise your intentions under the name of 'love' if you feel it will salve your conscience. I am proud of you."

Camilla had often wished to hear her mother proclaim pride for her. Usually she deflected compliments from others on Camilla's sewing or deportment or music with a "She may improve if she applies herself" or some other dismissive phrase. Yet to be praised for a perceived hypocrisy was horribly distasteful. Camilla wondered if she knew her mother at all. Certainly the headstrong Lolly Feldon who had made a runaway match, as Nanny Mallow had told her, was long since submerged in the calculating Mrs. Twainsbury. Understanding that her mother's worries were caused by a ne'er-do-well husband and the strains of raising two daughters creditably on next to no money did not reconcile Camilla to her mother's point of view.

She sat and listened to her mother talk about the glittering future Camilla would have. "But why are you still packing, Mama?"

"We cannot remain here any longer. Had I known Lady LaCorte was about to commence on her labor, I should have left this afternoon. Remaining as a guest in a house where there is to be a newborn infant is beyond the line of pleasing. If you were already married to Sir Philip, that would be a different matter. But as I am a stranger and your engagement is not yet given out, of course we shall depart in the morning."

"I see. Yes, of course."

"Speaking of engagements, have you a ring as yet?"

"No, we have not thought of such things."

"I suppose he won't be able to acquire any family pieces until after Lady LaCorte is recovered."

"I suppose not. Mama, may I leave you? I promised Tinarose I'd remain with her."

"Of course, my child. Come, kiss me." Mrs.

Twainsbury patted Camilla's cheek. "Don't look so distressed at a little plain speaking. I am, indeed, most proud of you."

"Thank you, but you have no cause."

The hours swept past in the silent house. The governess, returning with hot cocoa, reported that a vigil was being held in the servants' hall. Camilla tramped between nursery and library until the little girls fell asleep. Then she and Tinarose passed the time in the library playing piquet while Philip worked on his book. None of them wanted to go to bed, although Mrs. Twainsbury had retired after her wearying day of travel. No word came from the bedroom on the floor above.

Midnight passed, then one. Though Tinarose resisted going to bed, Camilla made her comfortable on the sofa, laying her large Norwich shawl over the girl. Philip threw another log onto the fire, then beckoned to Camilla. She smoothed Tinarose's forehead. "Try to sleep a little. I'll wake you the instant there's word."

"You're very good to me, 'Aunt' Camilla," Tinarose said with a hint of her mischievous smile.

"Call me that again and we shall pull caps." Camilla squeezed her hand and left her to reflection and sleep.

"Did you tell your mother?" Philip asked in an eager whisper.

"Yes. She reacted most oddly but seemed pleased."

"Oddly?"

"Yes. I shan't tell you how; it would flatter your vanity too much." She knew him well enough to know that he'd find her mother's conclusions amusing, but she didn't want to expose how little her mother knew *her.*

"But she consents?" he asked, putting his arm about her and encouraging her to put her head on his shoulder.

"I think so. She certainly seemed to like the idea of my marrying you. I wish, though, that she didn't wish to leave in the morning. I would like you two to become better acquainted."

"You're still leaving in the morning?"

"She feels, and rightly, that Lady LaCorte will have enough on her plate without adding guests, one of whom is perfectly unknown to her. If we were already married . . ." His arm tightened involuntarily, and she caught her breath at the look in his eyes.

"A pity one can't simply wake up the local parson and be married at once, for, I swear, I'd marry you tonight if I could."

She could only lean against him, enjoying the strength of his arms and his nearness. After a moment, she looked up into his eyes. "How goes the book?"

Between the lateness of the hour, the low light, and his difficult handwriting, Camilla found it necessary to rest her eyes. Letting her head fall back against the wing of the chair by the fire, she closed her eyes for only a second. When she opened them, the fire had dwindled to almost nothing. Disoriented, she struggled up, her hand to her head. "Philip?"

The knock that had awakened her was repeated. Over on the sofa, Tinarose raised herself on her elbow, blinking. "Is it morning?"

"Come in," Camilla called.

Dr. March poked his head in. Water droplets

sparkled like silver sequins in his bright hair. His shirt was open, waistcoat and cravat discarded during the night, the sleeves rolled back on his strong forearms. "Is Miss LaCorte here? Her mother is calling for her."

"Mama?" Tinarose swung her feet to the floor, the shawl falling away unheeded. "Is she . . . all right?"

"Of course," he said, unconsciously holding out his hand to her. She took it, her eyes focusing on his face, every thought concentrated on the patient upstairs. "She's perfectly well. Fourth children don't take very long as a rule."

"But it's been hours!"

"Only six. It's three o'clock in the morning."

"I must go at once," Tinarose said. Though she turned to go, she pressed his hand between hers for one grateful instant. "Thank you, Dr. March. Thank you."

When she rushed away, he wheeled as if to follow her, his hand still outstretched as though to draw her back again. Then he let it fall, but his gaze stayed with her until Camilla spoke.

"You look worn to a shadow, sir. A glass of something?"

"Philip promised me a glass of brandy. Where is he?"

"Here." His voice came from the hall. He came in, bearing three cups on a tray. "I heard my sister-in-law's maid come down some few minutes ago and thought the girls would like something to wake them up, but I see I'm too late."

"Not for me. What's that?"

"Cocoa but there's brandy in the library."

"Cocoa sounds good, though I don't recommend it as a rule. Too rich for the average constitution." When he tasted Mrs. Lamsard's cocoa, however, he seemed to forget his objections. He licked at the chocolate mustache left on his upper lip and stared with disbelief into the depths of the cup. "Food of the Gods," he muttered.

"Doctor," Camilla began, curious because no one else seemed to be. "Tell me about the baby."

"The baby?" he repeated, still bemused by what he was drinking. "Oh, perfectly healthy. Not too large and very lusty. No doubt you'll hear crying in the night. Lungs like a bellows."

"Thank God," Philip said.

"Yes, indeed," Camilla said. "Lady LaCorte must be so happy to be safely delivered."

"Nanny Mallow was a great help when her ladyship seemed to lose heart about halfway through the proceedings."

A rap at the door made them all look up. "Mama," Camilla said. "I'm sorry you were awakened."

"It's unimportant. I understand I am to congratulate you, Sir Philip, on the addition to your family."

"Thank you, Mrs. Twainsbury. But I'm not Sir Philip any longer. I've been replaced, thankfully, by young Sir Myron Thomas LaCorte, born this day, fourteen December, year of our Lord 1817. Long life to him."

"Amen," Camilla and the doctor said and clinked their cups together. Mrs. Twainsbury said nothing.

CHAPTER FOURTEEN

A week later, Camilla sat in her mother's clean parlor, listening to Sir John's son and young Mr. Van der Groot argue some fine point of Greek drama. They used a great many quotes, both in Greek and Latin. She thumbed through the recipe book on her lap, which Mrs. Lamsard had given her at her parting, and did not attend.

Finally, she caught a sound she had been waiting for—the whistle of Sir John himself, coming to collect his son on his way back from the village. Excusing herself with a smile, she left the room, not that the young men noticed.

"Your letters, Miss Twainsbury," Sir John said, his hair gleaming as white as the snow still clinging to the yew bushes either side of the doorway.

"Thank you, Sir John," Camilla said, holding the three or four envelopes tightly. "I hope you didn't go too far out of your way."

"Not at all. A pleasure. Is my son ready to go?"

"I think they've gotten as far as Sophocles."

Sir John sighed. "May I ask you a personal question, Miss Twainsbury?"

She blinked at him. Both the local magistrate and a noted proponent of preservation, he'd never given the slightest sign that he knew her from any of the other girls in the village. He was always civil, but rather absently so.

"Are you at all interested in Greeks or Romans and their ilk?"

She colored. "No, Sir John."

"I thought as much."

"My interest lies in medieval Ireland. I . . . took a fancy for it while I was away."

He raised one white eyebrow. "I shall not mention your confidence to my son. The constant Greek is bad enough. I can do without adding the Gaelic."

Camilla hastened to pour balm on the waters. "He's a very intelligent young man. I'm sure he must enjoy Oxford."

"I wish they'd teach him a few things about women," Sir John muttered.

"He is young yet."

Sir John nodded as if understanding the rejection behind her words. "He's been using your house as a coffee club. I never thought to ask if it discommoded you. I suppose I assumed you were pleased about it."

"It is my mother's house, sir, not mine."

"But it makes no difference to you whether he visits here or not."

"No, Sir John." She wished she could soften this by telling him that there was someone else, but her mother had forbidden it. "Besides, he soon forgets I'm here. I think he and Mr. Van der Groot will make great scholars. One day the world will marvel that two such men came from such a small village."

"I marvel all the time, Miss Twainsbury. I'll relieve you of having to do so."

As soon as they'd gone, Camilla put on her heaviest coat and boots and ran down to the garden shed, an extremely lonely spot in winter. Three of the letters were addressed to her mother, one of them in Nanny Mallow's writing. The fourth was for Camilla. At the sight of the all but illegible script, sprawling with energy across the buff-colored paper, Camilla closed her eyes and sent a grateful prayer skyward.

True, she probably shouldn't have gone behind her mother's back to achieve this letter. Yet for the past week, her mother had been using every stratagem to prevent Camilla from collecting the post, usually one of her more pleasant tasks. Even today, Mrs. Twainsbury had told her not to trouble herself, that she would collect it on her way back from visiting a sick neighbor.

Philip had promised faithfully to write every day, yet this was the first letter she'd seen. Though she had not asked, Camilla felt certain her mother was preventing his letters from reaching her. She ignored the niggling little fear at the back of her mind, the one that said Philip had already forgotten her.

> *My Dear Camilla:*
> *If I do not hear from you in response to this letter, I shall come myself. Your mother has written to me, telling me of the illness you contracted on your journey home. I will not wound you by telling you my opinion of this tale, but as an author, I feel it lacks that unstudied quality which is the hallmark of the best fiction. But whether you be in health or ill, whether you still love me or have discovered your mistake, I will come within three days.*
> *'Til forever, your Philip*

She clasped this missive to her bosom, feeling that last doubt drown under the swell of her happiness. Her mother might try stratagems and practice deceit, but there was no point and so she would tell her. Smoothing out the letter, she read it again and perceived this time that something was written on the back, in a rounder hand and with lighter ink.

"Camilla, come as soon as you can. We all miss you. Tinarose."

The three days passed. Camilla had not told her mother about Philip's letter or his impending visit. She felt her mother could easily invent some reason for them to be halfway across the country by the time he arrived. Though she'd handed her mother the letters, Mrs. Twainsbury only shot her a sharp glance to which Camilla responded with perfect blankness.

The third day came and went. Camilla slept at last, fitfully, her eyes too hot with tears to find much ease. When morning came, she awoke with a simple resolution in her mind. Dimly, across the fields in the frosty air, came the sound of the church's ancient bells, mellowly tolling the hour. "Seven o'clock," Camilla muttered. "I suppose the public coaches must run on Christmas Eve."

When her mother came home from doing the flowers in church for the night's service, Camilla took the empty basket from her and hung it on its proper hook. Then she put tea and luncheon on the table. "How is the vicar? Is his cough improved?"

"Very much. He'll be able to give his sermon today, I think." She reached out for the teapot but hesitated, her hand floating in air, as she saw the crumpled letter lying on the napkin. "What is this, Camilla?"

"A letter from Philip. Sir John was kind enough to bring it up from the village the other day. I asked him to do it."

"May I read it?"

"You've read the others," Camilla said.

"My goodness, what a headstrong young man. I shall see him when he comes today. There must be no more of this sort of thing."

"I quite agree. There won't be any more letters."

Her mother smiled and poured the tea. "I'm glad you are going to be sensible."

"I didn't say that, Mother. On the contrary, I intend to be magnificently nonsensical. I love Philip. No one has ever made me feel safe enough to risk everything."

"I suppose you know what you are talking about; I confess I do not. Safe enough to risk? What does that mean, may I ask?"

"It's hard to explain it to you. I know only one person who might understand."

"Your precious *Mister* LaCorte," her mother said sharply.

"No, that's not who I meant, though I'm sure he would understand. I meant a girl I heard of once—oh, how sweet she must have been. How wildly certain that love was worth any risk. Perhaps you remember her, Mother. She was called Lolly Feldon."

Mrs. Twainsbury's thin lips twitched. "I suppose Nanny Mallow told you all about my youth."

"Some of it. I know you made a runaway marriage and that you were cast off by my grandparents because of it."

"Yes. A sweet, romantic tale she made of it, I'm sure. She can't tell you the other side of it, but I can. I can tell you about living in squalid boarding-houses, never with anything to call your own because everything is up for pawn. And if you do, by some miracle, find yourself a little house where you can live decently, your husband comes home to tell you about some wonderful new opportunity in some distant town. So you leave whatever friends you've made and you travel with him to another squalid boardinghouse with a sluttish mistress and slovenly servants. Love dies in those places, my dear. It gets no light, no air, nothing but arid weariness."

Camilla came around to her mother's chair. "I don't expect you to believe me, Mother, but it won't be like that for us."

Mrs. Twainsbury laughed shortly. "That's what your father said when we ran away together." Then a ghost of a smile crossed her lips. "He never stopped hoping, your father. The next town was always Fairyland for him, a place where all his dreams would come true."

"You never need leave this house," Camilla said.

"Only because he died before he could move us again. It was coming; I could feel it whenever he spoke. I told him I wouldn't go with him anymore, but I knew I would. All he had to do was ask me, and I was still such a fool. . . ."

"That's how I feel about Philip, Mama. Wherever he wants me to go, I'll go."

"Don't be a fool, Camilla. I don't want that life for you. You don't know how hard it is. Scrimping and pinching, making one pound do for five, never beforehand with the world, always afraid of the bailiffs and the butcher. How I hated writing to my parents for money! They made me beg for every penny. If you marry a man of property, then you need never fear for your children."

"But, Mama, you've raised me to be a poor man's wife. Who knows more about making and mending than I? If Philip is really to have no title and no fortune, then I am all the more the perfect wife for him. But what matters most is that he is the perfect husband for me."

"Wait, then. Ask him for time when he comes. You are still so young. He'll give you time."

"I'm older than Lolly Feldon was, Mama. Besides, Philip isn't coming here."

"He isn't?" Mrs. Twainsbury said hopefully.

"No. He was supposed to have come yesterday, Mama. Look at the date on the letter."

"Doesn't that prove what I'm saying? Obviously he's thought it over and decided that it's best not to see you again. I honor him for it."

"I'm glad. Have you had all you wanted? Now, we must go or we'll miss the coach. Never mind about the dishes. I asked Mrs. Willet's oldest daughter to come by and close up the house."

"Coach? Close up the house? What do you mean, Camilla?" Mrs. Twainsbury came to her feet, still holding her daughter fast by the arm.

"I'm not going to let you make the same mistake your parents made, Mama," Camilla said, rubbing her cheek against her mother's. "Your traveling dress is laid out on your bed, and I've packed the small portmanteau for you. You had better hurry."

"I'm not going. Don't be ridiculous. You can't run after a man this way. Where is your pride? Listen to me, Camilla."

"Well, Mama, the way I look at it is this: You can stay here and think of lots of things to say to me. Or you can come with me on my elopement and say them to me face-to-face. Who knows? Perhaps you *can* talk me out of it."

Several hours later, arriving at the Red Knight Inn, Mrs. Twainsbury was barren of words. Camilla had turned them all away, gently but firmly. "We walk from here," she said. "Leave the baggage. Merridew will collect it later."

"Walk?" Mrs. Twainsbury said as if she'd never heard the term before.

"It's traditional. Come along." Camilla turned back as she went from the courtyard, remembering how Philip had stood and watched her go that first day. With the winter evening fast closing in, she almost felt she could see him.

The two women hadn't gone very far, however, when a coach and four came by. A few hundred yards past them, the coach pulled up and stood on the roadway, the horses steaming in the cold air. The door flew open. "May I offer you ladies a ride? It's too cold for walking."

Mrs. Twainsbury clutched Camilla's arm. "Don't talk to strange men," she whispered.

"No, of course not, Mama." She patted Mrs. Twainsbury's hand. "Thank you, sir. Do you know Savyard Manor? It's not far from here."

"I know it very well, indeed. By a curious coincidence, I'm heading there myself."

"Don't believe him," Mrs. Twainsbury said. "It's a ruse to get us in his power."

But something about that voice had sounded familiar. Deeper and much louder than Philip's, it had a ring to it not unlike his own. Perhaps it was no more than a common accent. Camilla came on, her mother leaden-footed behind her.

A face nearly black with sunburn looked out from the carriage, topped with hair the color of new iron. He wore ordinary gentleman's clothing but characterized by extreme neatness, even though one sleeve was pinned to the shoulder. A smart valet climbed out and helped the ladies into the coach.

"Who are you, sir?" Mrs. Twainsbury quavered.

"I think I know," Camilla said.

"Do you?" The dark eyes were very much like Philip's but even more crinkled when he beamed at her. "Then you have the advantage of me, Miss . . . ?"

"Miss Twainsbury," she said with a laugh. "Miss Camilla Twainsbury but not, I hope, for long. I hope to change it for LaCorte quite soon."

The dark eyes narrowed. "Other girls have hoped for that, but I only knew of one that achieved it. Yet, why do I have a strong suspicion that another LaCorte male is doomed to lose his freedom?"

"He might marry, sir, but he'll lose nothing by it."

Drawn by horses, powerful even when weary, Camilla arrived at the Manor long before she'd hoped. Samson opened the door. "Is Mister Philip at home?" she asked, breathless now that she'd be seeing him in moments.

"Why, Miss Twainsbury," Samson said, looking past her at the coach. "Mr. Philip is . . ." Then the butler completely forgot training and decorum. Pushing past her, he went running down the stairs as he'd probably not run in years.

"Oh, sir! Oh, sir."

Camilla entered the house, looking everywhere at once. Nothing had changed, and she was glad of it. There was still a faint scent of flowers in the air and well-loved furniture. She hurried to the library and opened the door.

The fire was cold ashes, the candles fresh and new, wicks as white as an unwritten page. The ink in the pot on the desk was untouched and the pen uncut. Looking at the manuscript pages on the desk, Camilla saw that Philip had written hardly a word since she'd left, though he'd crossed a good many out with savage slashes of his pen.

Worried now, Camilla tore up the staircase, heading for the nursery. Tinarose must know where her uncle could be. On the landing, making the turn to go up, Camilla collided with Philip, just emerging from his sister-in-law's chamber.

"Camilla?" he said, his hands tight on her shoulders.

"Oh, you are here," she said.

"Yes. And so are you." He spoke slowly, unemotionally like a man in the grip of exhaustion. Perhaps she would have worried that he wasn't glad to see her, but his hands betrayed his true feelings. They held her so tightly that she bore the marks of them a day later.

"What is it? What's wrong? I knew when you didn't come that something must be amiss."

"Is it Christmas Eve already? I suppose I have lost track of the days. My nephew is ill."

"Oh, no. What is it?"

A ghost of a chuckle escaped his lips. "Croup. Just croup, Nanny Mallow says, but Beulah won't let go of the child. She says she knows he's going to die, and nothing anyone can say seems to change her mind. Even Evelyn can't get her to give him the baby. If they can take the boy, they can treat him, but she won't give him to them."

"Wait here," Camilla said, freeing herself. "Wait here."

Philip smiled as he closed his eyes, leaning tiredly against the wall. After two days without sleep, even the wall felt comfortable.

Camilla had come. How like her not to be swayed by dark circumstances into believing the worst of him, even though he felt sure her mother had poured poison enough into her ears. He promised himself never to take advantage of her faith in him. Idly, waiting for her, he wondered

how soon they could marry. A quiet family service
would be best. He could almost see the church,
glowing with the lights of many candles, as Camilla
came down the flower-bedecked aisle. She had
rather heavy footsteps for such a light creature. It
sounded as if she was wearing thick boots under
her wedding gown.

"Philip, old man," someone said, and Philip knew
he was dreaming, for that voice had been stilled by
waves half a world away.

"Myron?" he said.

"Yes, old man. It's me. Wake up, do."

"Myron!" Philip jerked awake, clutching at the
man before him, staring with astounded eyes. "My
God, they said . . . What in heaven's name happened to you? Where's your arm?"

"Buried on an island. It was the arm or me, but
that's a long tale for a winter's evening. This young
lady says my Beulah is ill. Where is she?"

Philip opened the bedroom door and stood in
the opening, his arm tight around Camilla. Sir
Myron went down on one knee before the arm-
chair that held his wife. Lady LaCorte looked just
as usual, except that her abundant hair lay loose
around her shoulders. Yet every few seconds long
shudders passed through her body, shaking her
and setting her teeth to chattering. Against her
bosom, clutched tight, she held her child. "He's
going to die, Doctor," she said, not looking at this
stranger who had entered. "I've lost my husband,
and now I'm going to lose my son. I just know it."

"You haven't lost anything, Beulah. I'm here."
Captain LaCorte lifted her chin with his fingers.
For a moment, she stared; then she looked away,
closing her eyes. She pressed her trembling fingertips to the center of her forehead. "I really am

mad," she said. "I've heard the voices whisper it when they thought I couldn't hear, but it's true."

"No, it isn't. I always told you I'd come back to you, no matter what stood in my way. Am I a liar, Beulah?"

She laughed. "You always were."

"Let me see my son."

Her arm fell away a little from her body, and Captain LaCorte took his child in his arm. "A fine boy," he said, nodding to Nanny Mallow, who was already there to take the child. As she hurried away, Camilla was relieved beyond speech to hear the baby cough.

Philip's arm about her shoulder drew her back out of the room. "They'll be all right now. Where do you suppose he came from? Former king of a cannibal isle, if I know Myron. Or maybe he was taken to safety by the lost islanders of Atlantis. Wouldn't surprise me a bit."

"Ahem," Camilla said. Going up on tiptoe, she surprised him with a kiss. He didn't hesitate long before taking command of it. "That's what I wanted to know," she said with a sigh. "Go and dress yourself in your finest attire," she added. "It's Christmas Eve, and we have much to be thankful for."

Several hours later, gaiety infused every inch of the common rooms. The greenery that the stable lads had hoarded was brought in with suitable revelry and hung in boughs over windows and doors. The kissing balls the maids had been working on were hung in spots most likely to bring their prey to doom while Samson lit candles with a wild lack of worry over their cost. Mrs. Twainsbury found herself in the kitchen, drinking an amazingly mellow cup of chocolate while watching Mrs. Lamsard create a feast out of seemingly nothing.

As for Camilla and Philip, he followed her from room to room as she bustled about the small tasks of Christmas. Every time she passed beneath mistletoe, he kissed her, echoed by screams of delight from Nell and Grace, who followed him, urging him to "do it again, Uncle Philip," and racing away every time he threatened to kiss one of them. Camilla found herself working less and loitering more under the cunningly wrought balls of holly and ivy, ribbons and baubles, the branch of mistletoe hanging beneath.

"Aren't you supposed to take a berry each time?" she asked.

"If I do that, soon there are no more berries and no more kisses," he said.

"Oh. I see. That is something to worry about."

"Not for you," he said, kissing her again. "Never for you."

When the waits came to sing in the darkness beyond the lamps by the front door, everyone in the house who could came to listen. As the voices, man and woman's, boy and girl's, rang out and faded into the distance of the stars, Camilla leaned her head on Philip's shoulder and let the peace of the season fill her heart and soul. Wherever time would take them, whatever fate brought them, she didn't need to fear that she'd ever lose her home. Love was her home, and she carried it with her.

More Regency Romance
From Zebra